A Note to Readers

In *Maggie's Choice*, we meet Rob Allerton's three children: Ethan, Maggie, and Cuyler. While the Allertons and their friends are fictional characters, the events they find themselves surrounded by are not.

In 1744 and 1745, the Great Awakening, a revival that swept through the American Colonies, was at its peak, led by the Reverend Jonathan Edwards (who also appears in this book). While many of the first English settlers in New England had left their homes either because of a desire for religious freedom or because they wanted to tell Native Americans about Jesus, many of their descendents over one hundred years later did not know what it meant to have a personal relationship with Jesus. Going to church was simply something good people were supposed to do. Jonathan Edwards and other leaders of that time were used by God to "awaken" the people to a personal love for Jesus.

Maggie's Choice also reminds us that slavery was common in the Northern colonies, as well as in the South. Although there were always some people who fought against the evil of slavery, it took two hundred years and a Civil War before slavery was outlawed in our country.

MAGGIE'S CHOICE

Norma Jean Lutz

PUBLISHING, INC.

Uhrichsville, Ohio

© MCMXCVII by Barbour Publishing, Inc.

ISBN 1-57748-145-3

Published by Barbour Publishing, Inc.
P.O. Box 719
Uhrichsville, Ohio 44683
http://www.barbourbooks.com

ecpa Member of the
Evangelical Christian
Publishers Association

Printed in the United States of America.

Cover illustration by Chris Cocozza.
Inside illustrations by Adam Wallenta.

CHAPTER ONE

The Launch

Maggie Allerton struggled to restrain the excitement bubbling up inside her. Her younger brother, Cuyler, at age eight, could run about the Foy Shipyard with abandoned glee. But at age twelve, she was expected to use decorum befitting a lady. The moment their father, Dr. Robert Allerton, pulled their small black carriage to a halt, Cuyler leaped down and began running and hopping about.

Maggie wished she could run right alongside him. Instead, she waited for her father to secure the harnesses and come around to help her down. Controlling her hoops while getting in and out of a carriage was a skill she'd not yet perfected.

She landed lightly, then reached up to be sure her straw bonnet was secure. Decorated with bright blue ribbons and new feathers, the made-over hat was as stylish as any in Boston. Maggie's nanny, Martha Lankford, said so. Martha assured Maggie that blue was the best color to go with Maggie's copper-colored hair. Martha's opinion meant a great deal to Maggie—not only was Martha the Allerton's nanny, she was also the best seamstress in the city.

The launching of a new ship provided a great deal of excitement for the city of Boston. In fact, the citizens turned the event into a holiday. Even Maggie's older brother, Ethan, was given the afternoon off from his accounting books at the counting house of the Foy Shipping Line.

"Look!" Cuyler called out. "It's the governor's carriage! Zounds! What a fancy carriage. Wish ours looked like that."

"Cuyler," Maggie warned, "watch your language." She glanced about, hoping no one had heard. To her father she said, "Good thing Mother isn't here to hear him talk like that."

"If your mother were alive, Margaret," said Dr. Allerton, "I'm sure she'd keep a tighter rein on him than you or I, either one."

Her brother was right about Governor William Shirley's carriage. There were few carriages in all of Boston as elaborate as his. Other shipping merchants such as the Truesdales and the Clarkes also owned ornate carriages which were shipped over from England. And of course, their Uncle Thomas drove about town in the stylish carriage left to him by his late father, Josiah Foy.

Her father offered his arm, and Maggie hooked her gloved hand in the crook of it as they strolled through the bustling crowd. "It appears as though all of Boston has turned out for this launch," her father said as he gently guided her along.

Suddenly, Cuyler's attention was turned in a new direction. "There's Ethan!" he exclaimed, pointing down the wharf to where the new ship, *Thetis*, stood tall and proud. "And Uncle Thomas is with him." Without waiting for his father's permission, Cuyler sprinted through the crowd toward his older brother and uncle.

"I hope he doesn't injure anyone," Maggie quipped.

Her father chuckled. "One would think he hadn't seen Ethan at breakfast this very morning."

As they talked, Maggie glanced about to see if her friends, Susannah Clarke and Dancy Truesdale, had yet arrived. Following the launch, she would be a guest for high tea at the Clarke home, and Dancy would be there as well. Maggie was looking forward to the gaiety of the afternoon more so even than the launch.

The towering ship stood silently waiting, resting in its giant cradle made of wooden stocks. Workers were busy greasing the timbers that ran in back of the ship into the water. This would allow the ship to glide out easily from the stocks.

The air was filled with the aroma of fresh-cut pine. Stacks of honey-colored lumber lay about the area ready to be used to finish the interior cabinet work on this ship or to be part of Uncle Thomas's next project. Maggie's industrious uncle, who was stepbrother to her father, was always busy in some new venture. In spite of the pockmarks on his face, he was quite handsome. He cut an imposing figure as he stood greeting the citizens of Boston and awaiting the magic moment of the launch.

"Good day, Maggie, Robert," he called to them as they approached. "Didn't I tell you this one would be in the water before 1743 was out?"

"That you did, Thomas, that you did," Maggie's father agreed. "But it's not under sail quite yet." He wet his finger and put it up to the wind. "This cool wind tells me we'll have an early winter. Perhaps you'll be iced in before she's fully loaded."

Maggie knew her father was joking. The breeze off Boston Harbor was quite balmy for late September.

Uncle Thomas knew it was a joke as well. "Not much you'd know about launching weather or sailing weather either, Dr. Allerton," he said with a smile. "A ship would be in great peril with you at the helm."

"The very reason I leave all this frivolity to you, Thomas," Father said with a wave of his hand. That wave indicated not only the Foy Shipyards, but also the nearby Foy Shipping Line offices and extensive warehouses on Long Wharf. Maggie's uncle owned them all.

Cuyler was leaning back, gazing up at the ship. "It's so big!" he said.

"But not my biggest," Uncle Thomas retorted.

"The biggest is the *Stamitos*, which is on a return trip from Barbados just now," fourteen-year-old Ethan told them.

Uncle Thomas gave Ethan a smile and slapped his shoulder playfully. "That's right, Ethan." To Maggie's father he said, "This boy's a natural as a ship merchant. I'll wager he knows where nearly every Foy ship is just now and when it's due to return."

Maggie was proud of her brother, who looked striking in his russet greatcoat with the swirls of gold braid and decorative brass buttons down the front. The same gold braid was repeated on his cocked tricorn hat. Large sleeves folded back revealed crisp ruffles at his wrists. Although Ethan cared little about his fancy wardrobe, Uncle Thomas required that Ethan dress like a dandy for work each day.

"He's a bright boy all right," her father was saying in agreement. "Much better in the shipping business than I."

"Most anyone would be better in the shipping business than you, Robert," Uncle Thomas teased.

"But who calls me when they're sick?" her father retorted.

The two of them teased one another mercilessly. Hearing it so much, Maggie had grown used to it. "Where's Aunt Ruth?" Maggie wanted to know.

"Feeling poorly," her uncle replied. "We felt it was best for her to rest."

Maggie wasn't surprised. Aunt Ruth was a small, pale lady who seemed sad much of the time. Over the past few years, she'd given birth to four babies, all of whom died. The heartbreak and grief had been too much for her.

Just then a rumble of wheels sounded from behind them. They whirled around to see a carriage coming right down the wharf. People scattered out of the way.

"Only Winston Clarke would ride through the crowd to be seen by all," Ethan quipped. "And take a look at his new calash."

Maggie admired the new low-slung carriage with low wheels and a collapsible top. Not even Governor Shirley had one like this. As the carriage came to a halt midway down the wharf, the liveried footman stepped down to open the door for the Clarke family.

"May I go see Susannah?" Maggie asked her father.

"Of course," he answered, releasing her arm. "You go on."

Not only did the Clarke family have a new carriage, but

Susannah was arrayed in a lavish plum-colored silk dress piped in dark velvet. A stunning matching hat topped out the ensemble. Amid such finery, Maggie felt a trifle awkward. Thankfully, the feeling lasted only a moment, for Susannah had spotted her.

"Maggie! There you are, Maggie. Isn't this all so exciting? I love celebrations, don't you?" Susannah allowed the footman to assist her to the ground. "You are still coming to high tea this afternoon, are you not?" She smoothed her skirts with her white kid gloves as she glanced about. "Is Dancy here yet? Oh, we're going to have such a delightful time together."

Maggie laughed at her friend's chatter. "In answer to all your questions: I love celebrations, I'm still coming, and Dancy's not arrived."

"Good day, Margaret," Susannah's mother said as she swept gracefully from the carriage step to the ground. "Susannah does chatter like a little squirrel, doesn't she?" Pert Clarke carefully adjusted the full skirts of her gown, which was every bit as lovely as her daughter's. "I dare say, I wonder how you put up with her."

Before Maggie could comment, Mrs. Clarke continued, "Your uncle seems to have commandeered the attention of every citizen in Boston. I'm amazed at this crowd."

Susannah grabbed Maggie's arm. "Come, Maggie. Let's hurry down to where your uncle and father are. We don't want to miss a thing! Oh, and there's Ethan."

Maggie noticed Susannah's voice always rose a bit when she was anywhere near Ethan, which didn't happen very often. Maggie knew that Ethan viewed the Clarke business as competition in the shipping industry, but it was more than that. He appeared to try to avoid Susannah altogether.

"Come, Mother," Susannah said over her shoulder.

Winston Clarke was already down the wharf at the launch site involved in animated conversation with Uncle Thomas. Maggie was astonished that he would leave his wife's side, forcing her to walk alone. Her father would never have done that to her mother. Although Maggie was only four when her mother had died, she remembered many details about the red-haired, Irish immigrant Kathleen Allerton.

The workers had finished greasing the ramp, and it was nearly time for the launch. The girls hurried to join the group clustered nearest the ship. Polite greetings were made all around, and true to form, as soon as Ethan had given Susannah a polite hello, he moved some distance away.

Just before time for the launch, petite Dancy Truesdale came tripping toward them. Maggie waved. "Dancy, thank goodness you've arrived. They're preparing to knock out the forms."

"I'm so glad we didn't miss anything," she told them, quite out of breath. "The new baby was fussing, and Mother couldn't decide whether to bring him along or leave him with the nurse."

Lydia Truesdale with her husband, Joseph, soon joined the group, and Mrs. Truesdale did indeed hold the baby in her arms.

Just then, Susannah leaned over to Maggie. "What's that in your brother's hand?" she asked.

Thinking Susannah meant Ethan, Maggie looked in his direction. "Nothing that I see."

"No, no. Your younger brother."

"Oh, Cuyler? That's his garden snake, Beagan."

Susannah released a loud gasp. "A live snake?"

"Beagan?" Dancy said. "He *named* a snake?"

"It means 'little one' in Irish," Maggie told them. "Cuyler takes him most everywhere."

Hearing his name, Cuyler skipped over to them. "You wanted

11

to see Beagan?" He proudly held up the wriggling little critter, and Susannah and Dancy both jumped back.

"Ugh! Get that nasty thing away from me!" Susannah protested. She spread her fan and put it to her face as though to protect herself.

"It's only a little garden snake," Cuyler said, stepping closer. "If you look real close you can see all the pretty designs."

Dancy squealed and jumped behind Maggie.

"I guess you'd better put him back in your pocket for now," Maggie told him. She'd often played with garden snakes—and toads as well—when she was younger. It never occurred to her to be frightened.

At the sound of the commotion, Dr. Allerton turned around. Seeing the problem, he motioned for Cuyler to come back to his side.

"All safe," Maggie told them.

"Thank goodness," Susannah said with a sigh.

Uncle Thomas provided a blessed interruption as he climbed up on a section of scaffolding and called out for the people's attention. He prayed a short prayer over the *Thetis*, asking God to watch over her and protect her while she was under sail. The governor gave a short speech, followed by another speech by one of the magistrates. At last, Thomas Foy called out, "Release the supports!"

Hammers banged as the forms were knocked out of the way. Other workers stood at the sides to push, giving the heavy bulk the boost it needed to commence sliding. Wild cheers went up as the ship picked up momentum, and slid down quickly and easily, ending with a monstrous splash into Boston Harbor. Seagulls shrieked and wheeled about overhead, joining in the noisy event.

Maggie gasped and clung to her friends as the men scurried

about to pull ropes and bring the now-launched ship firmly into the dock before it could float away. She felt she couldn't breathe until the vessel was secured on the far side of the dock. The Boston selectmen and magistrates formally shook Uncle Thomas's hand and congratulated him on the successful launch. There was much bustling about and what Maggie's father called "hobnobbing."

"Ships are so thrilling," Susannah was saying. "They can take a person to exciting far-off lands. Of course, when we came over from England I suffered terribly from seasickness, but I'm sure one would get used to it eventually. I believe the sailors call it getting your 'sea legs.' Funny saying, isn't it? Sea legs?"

The girls giggled as they walked along. The crowd began to thin out as people slowly strolled back to their carriages.

"Say, I have an idea," Susannah said, pulling them to a halt. "Let's ask if you two can ride back to our house in our carriage."

"That would be great fun," Maggie agreed.

Dancy nodded. "Let's ask."

Maggie turned about to see her father and Cuyler still talking with Ethan and Uncle Thomas. She hurried back to his side. "Father!" she called out excitedly. "May I ride to the Clarkes' home in their new carriage?"

Father smiled at her. "I see no reason why not. We'll see you there."

She tiptoed to reach up and kiss her father's cheek. "Oh, thank you, Father."

"I want to go in the new carriage," Cuyler piped up. "Let me go too."

"No, Cuyler," her father said. "This is just for Maggie and her friends."

"Not fair!" Cuyler stuck his lower lip out in a pout.

"Come on, Cuyler," Ethan said, "you can ride with me and Uncle Thomas in his carriage."

While Cuyler's attention was diverted, Maggie turned to rejoin her friends.

"Dancy can come with us," Susannah called out to Maggie. "Can you?"

"Yes," Maggie called back. "Father says it's fine."

As she hurried back toward her friends, a young girl emerged from the crowd. Her hair was disheveled beneath a soiled mob-cap, and her drab, threadbare dress hung limply to her ankles. Maggie judged her to be a year or so older than Cuyler. The girl gazed wide-eyed as though she were soaking in the beauty and finery about her. Then she spied Maggie, and Maggie could feel the girl admiring the ruffles and lace of her best Sunday dress. As Maggie drew nearer, the girl stood as though transfixed.

Suddenly, Maggie felt a yank on her arm. Susannah had grabbed her. "Don't touch that girl," she said in a loud whisper, as she dragged Maggie out around the young girl. "Don't you know? Her mother keeps company!"

Maggie knew that meant the mother had men come into her home. But what did that have to do with this little girl? As Maggie was assisted up into the fine calash, she gave one glance back, and her eyes locked with the sad eyes of the forlorn girl.

CHAPTER TWO
High Tea

There was plenty of room in the calash for all three girls and Susannah's parents. The ride to the Clarke home at the edge of Boston Common was a delight with the open top and the breeze blowing on them. Susannah and her mother held up face masks to protect their skin from the sun and wind. The girls chattered and giggled the entire way.

The stately three-story Clarke house was surrounded by dozens of carriages. Many guests had already arrived for high tea.

Clusters of footmen, dressed in smartly tailored liveries, gathered about, visiting together beneath a large shade tree in the yard.

"You girls may have your tea served in the upstairs nursery if you like," Pert Clarke said as the carriage stopped. "I'll have the servants serve you there."

"How wonderful, Mother," said Susannah. She turned to Maggie and Dancy. "Our own private tea party. What fun!"

The double parlors of the Clarke home had been opened by pushing back moving partitions. The guests milled about, laughing and visiting as tea was served on silver trays by the Clarkes' servants. A servant at the door took the girls' cloaks.

Governor Shirley and all the magistrates were there, arrayed in curled, powdered wigs and brightly colored greatcoats. Lilting melodies filled the room as a gentleman played the spinet at the far end of the room.

If this were an evening party rather than a tea, Maggie was certain the guests would be dancing. She'd heard that the Clarkes entertained often with evening dances, and it made her wish she knew how to dance.

Winston and Pert Clarke were courteous hosts and insisted that Susannah greet as many guests as possible before going to the nursery. Maggie watched as Susannah graciously mingled and chatted, giving little curtseys and extending her hand to the gentlemen.

Maggie wasn't sure she'd be able to do all that if it were required of her. Anyway, she couldn't imagine her father giving such a large party. First of all, their house wouldn't hold them all, but secondly, Dr. Allerton didn't think much of Boston's growing social scene. Even now, he was sitting off in a corner alone. Maggie realized he'd probably agreed to come only because of her. If Mother had not died, if Father had his lovely Kathleen by his side, Maggie knew everything might be different.

Just then, Susannah appeared and began ushering both Maggie and Dancy up the wide curving stairs. "Hurry, before Mother thinks of something else," Susannah giggled as she lifted her skirts and hurried up the steps with Maggie and Dancy in her wake. They scurried down the long hall into an alcove which opened into the spacious, sunny nursery.

Maggie had been in the Clarke home on one other occasion and was quite taken with its enormous size. The family often had friends from Salem—other shipping merchants—visit, and during those visits, parties occurred almost nightly. Martha Lankford often quipped, "There was no hoity-toity in Boston until the Clarkes arrived."

In the Allerton house, the nursery looked like a nursery, but Susannah's nursery looked like a sitting room. Maggie wondered what Susannah would think of Cuyler's blocks, tops, and toy soldiers being stacked on the shelves and his large rocking horse sitting right in the middle of the room.

Susannah arranged three delicately cushioned chairs in a circle around a small Pembroke table spread with a plaid cloth. "I'm overjoyed to have my very own company today," she told them. "Now that Michael and Oliver have left for Harvard, the house is so dreadfully dull. You've not met my brothers yet, have you? They're such great fun. Here, please sit down and I'll ring for our tea." She tugged at a tasseled bellpull near the door as Maggie and Dancy sat down, arranging their hoops carefully.

Before Susannah could be seated, a soft tapping sounded at the door. "Mercy. How could they get up here that fast? Winged feet?"

As she opened the door, there stood Cuyler, leaning against the door frame. A strangled gasp came from Susannah. "You still have that—that slimy reptile?"

"Yup. But Beagen's safe in my pocket."

Maggie was mortified, "Cuyler, what do you want?"

"Can I come and be with you, Maggie?" he said, looking past Susannah. "I don't want to stay downstairs."

"How did you know where I was?" Maggie demanded.

"I'm mighty good at tracking and following. I'd make a good Indian, wouldn't I?"

"Cuyler, go away. This is just for us girls," Maggie ordered, trying not to appear unkind. She didn't want the girls to think she was hateful, but she knew they didn't want a little brother bothering them.

"Oh, please, Maggie. I won't hurt anything. I promise I'll keep Beagan in my pocket. And if he crawls out I'll put him right back in."

Dancy gave a shudder. "How ghastly," she said.

Maggie rose and went to the door. "I apologize for the inter-ruption, Susannah. Excuse me a moment." Stepping into the alcove, she closed the door, then took her little brother by the shoulders. "Cuyler, you're causing me a great deal of embarrass-ment," she said softly. "Now go on downstairs with Father and leave me alone."

"Father is just sitting. I don't want to just sit."

"Where's Ethan?"

Cuyler shrugged. "Outside somewhere. He said he didn't care to come in." He pulled Beagan out and let the little snake crawl through his fingers.

"You must put your snake away while you're here. You saw how the girls reacted—other ladies may do the same. Now go find Ethan." It was just like Ethan not to come in. She had one brother who wouldn't mingle socially and another who wouldn't

18

leave her alone. What a disaster!

"But no one is serving sweetcakes outdoors." Cuyler's shoulders sagged a little.

"You're being impossible," Maggie said, becoming more and more flustered. "You must go back down and leave me alone." Gently, she guided him down the hall to the open balcony overlooking the double parlors. From that vantage point she waved to get her father's attention. It took a moment, but when she finally caught his eye, she pointed at Cuyler. Dr. Allerton quickly came to the foot of the stairs.

"Cuyler, come down here this moment," he said firmly.

"Not fair," Cuyler spouted as he hurried down the curving steps to his father.

Maggie heaved a little sigh. Finally she could be with her friends. By the time she returned to the nursery, the two servants were bustling about, setting the tea things on the table. A tea service of blue and gold sat primly on a black-and-gold Chinese tea tray. The silver cake basket, full of sweetcakes, wafers, and tiny sandwiches, was placed next to the tea service.

"I'm so sorry," Maggie said as she sat at her place. "I don't know what got into him."

"I'm sure he wouldn't have hurt anything," Dancy said.

"Oh, now," Susannah said, gracefully pulling off her kid gloves, "we certainly don't need a little one pestering us." She lifted the cake basket and passed it to Maggie. "Now if it'd been your older brother, that might have been different." She gave a wink, and Maggie was shocked. This girl was quite forward.

"Shall I pour?" asked one of the servants. The girl was not many years older than Susannah.

"Oh, mercy me, no," Susannah said with a wave of her hand. "None of you colonists know how to pour properly."

"Yes ma'am." Maggie could tell the girl was not a little embarrassed.

"Susannah!" Dancy spoke up. "Shame on you."

"Well, it's the truth. Mother and Father haven't been able to employ decent help since we left London. No one here has been trained properly."

"Will there be anything else, ma'am?" the girl asked, inching toward the door.

"No, Hayley. You may go."

When the servants had departed, Susannah poured the tea into thin cups decorated in pink rosebud designs. "It's true what I said, girls. Mother and Daddy have searched every nook and cranny of Boston for trained help, and it simply can't be found."

Maggie wasn't sure what to say since her family didn't have a single servant. Sometimes Martha hired girls to come in and help pluck the geese or do spring cleaning, but that was temporary.

"Our servants seem to do fine," Dancy put in as she took her cup and sipped from it.

Maggie did likewise but was fearful the fragile little cup might crumble right in her fingers. When the cake basket was passed, Maggie chose a golden sponge cake which looked soft as a cloud.

"And such odd servants we get," Susannah went on. "Take Hayley for instance." She leaned forward slightly, raising her eyebrows. "She's a revivalist!"

"No!" Dancy said with a soft little gasp. "Is she really?"

Before Maggie could catch herself, she blurted out, "What's a revivalist?"

"You mean you don't know?" Susannah touched her forehead. "You live here in Boston and you don't know what a revivalist is?"

20

Before Maggie could answer, Dancy explained, "They follow the itinerant preachers, Maggie. The ones who hold wild meetings—which they say are religious—in barns."

"In a barn or right outdoors in a pasture," Susannah added. "Can you feature such irreverence? A dirty old barn—to hold church?"

"The people become quite agitated, I'm told." Dancy wiped her fingers on the white linen napkin and reached for a slice of fruitcake.

"Very agitated," Susannah agreed. "Like this." She set down her cup and threw back her head. Touching her forehead with her hand she gave a loud groan. "Oh, I feel it, I feel it. Ooh, I feel the Spirit."

Maggie giggled with glee at the sight of the lovely Susannah acting out such a part.

"Or like this," Dancy said. Jumping up from her chair she knelt down and began to beat her breast, crying, "Oh, save me, save me! Please save me. I need to be saved."

"Then they jump up and down, waving their arms!" Susannah leaped to her feet to demonstrate. As the pantomimes continued, the three girls were consumed with fits of giggles until they could barely breathe beneath their whalebone corsets.

"I shall never have to wonder what a revivalist is after that demonstration," Maggie said, dabbing at her eyes with her kerchief. She'd laughed so hard, tears filled her eyes.

"Really, it's quite vile," Dancy said as she tried to catch her breath. "My father says they are completely in error."

"And my father calls them the 'bumbling backwoodsmen,' " Susannah said. "He feels they should be run out of any town they dare come into."

"They must be pretty bad," Maggie said thoughtfully. She

helped herself to another sandwich.

"Very bad," Dancy said. "They have absolutely no reverence for the church."

"I can tell you one thing," Susannah said, "you'll never catch me going near one of their wild heathenistic meetings. Why, even Pastor Gee of North Church will have nothing to do with them. And both Michael and Oliver say all the professors at Harvard are dead set against them."

A tap on the door interrupted their little party. "Girls!" came Mrs. Clarke's voice. "Sorry to interrupt your merrymaking, but guests are leaving and Dr. Allerton is asking for Maggie."

"Oh, Maggie, I wish you didn't have to leave so soon." Susannah rose to give Maggie a hug. "It was a pure pleasure having you."

"I enjoyed every minute, Susannah," Maggie told her. "Thank you for such a charming tea party."

"It was rompish good fun," Dancy agreed, also giving a hug. "Let's do it again soon."

The girls tripped down the stairs to find the parlor nearly empty. Ethan was waiting at the door for Maggie. "It's about time," he said under his breath. "I'm quite ready to leave."

"Just a moment. My wrap."

Suddenly Susannah was beside them, holding Maggie's cloak. "Ethan, how good that you could come to our home. Do come again, won't you?"

"As I find opportunity," he said, bowing stiffly then replacing his tricorn hat. "Maggie, please. Father's waiting."

Maggie was attempting to tie on her hat while Ethan was putting her cloak about her. "Give me a chance to tie my hat," she protested. But Ethan was bundling her right out the door and down the steps to the waiting carriage.

"Really, Father," Maggie complained once she was seated beside him in the carriage, "both my brothers were impossible today. Do you know how that makes me appear to Susannah and her parents?"

Dr. Allerton clucked at his team of bays. "I dare say, I probably wasn't much better. I nearly fell asleep in the corner."

"There, you see?" said Ethan. "Father doesn't care for the Clarkes any more than I do."

"I just wanted to eat with you," Cuyler chimed in.

Maggie moaned. "I like Susannah and Dancy, and I long to be invited again, but how can I if the three of you act like awkward misfits?"

"She's right, boys. We owe her an apology."

"I'm sorry, Maggie," said Ethan.

"Me too," Cuyler echoed.

Dr. Allerton put his arm around her. "And I apologize as well. Perhaps we should have insisted that Martha come along. Martha would have seen to it that the three of us behaved more gentlemanly!"

"That she would," Maggie agreed.

Even though Maggie loved Martha with all her heart, it was times like these when she wished her own mother were still alive. As they left the area of Boston Common and drove up Hanover Street to Copp's Hill, Maggie thought back over her delightful time at the tea party. How she wished she could have tea parties every day.

If she socialized more, perhaps she would know about such things as the revivalists. She wouldn't have admitted this to the girls, but they made her a bit curious about these strange services. What could the revivalists possibly have done to cause so much anger and mistrust?

CHAPTER THREE
Washday Blues

"You're attacking that candlestick as though you were attempting to kill it," Martha said with a chuckle. Her jolly face, as usual, was bright and smiling.

Maggie was sitting at the wooden kitchen table, polishing the brass candlesticks. They stood in a row on the table, waiting their turns to be polished to a high sheen. "I thought you were tending the laundry kettle," Maggie said.

"I came in to see how near done you were. I'll need help as

soon as you can come out."

"Yes, ma'am," she answered, her voice sullen.

"What a blessing that we can still do the wash outdoors. I pray the mild autumn weather lasts." Martha stepped into the pantry off the kitchen and came back out with the soap bar in hand and a knife for grating it. "Old man winter will drive me inside much too soon for my liking." When Maggie didn't answer, Martha moved toward the back door. "Hurry then, will you please?"

"Yes, ma'am." Helping with the laundry meant hauling several buckets of water from the well to the wash pot, then wringing out the clothes, which became heavy and bulky when wet.

At the door, Martha paused. "You seem distracted this morning. Are you coming down with something?"

"I'm fine."

"You look a bit paltry. I'll tell your Father when he comes home. You may be in need of a tonic." The door closed on her last words.

Maggie wasn't sure a tonic would help. She was sound in body, but something deep inside wasn't quite right. As she polished the candlesticks, she wondered who cleaned up melted wax and polished the candlesticks at the Clarke home. But she didn't really have to wonder. She knew for a fact it wasn't Susannah. Perhaps it was the girl named Hayley—the one who went to the wild barn meetings.

Once the brass candlesticks were shiny, Maggie firmed a candle down into each one. The burned wick of each candle was trimmed off in preparation for the evening's use. Martha was strict about the candles being prepared first thing each morning. "You don't wait until dark to prepare for the darkness," she'd say. Then she always added, "Likewise, don't wait until you're at death's door to prepare for departure."

Martha had a saying for everything. When Maggie was a little

25

girl, she'd loved all Martha's quaint sayings. Now they seemed aged and yellowed like some of the books in Father's study. She couldn't imagine the lovely Pert Clarke ever uttering such antiquated sayings.

When the candlesticks were finished, Maggie set them on a tray and placed the tray on a pantry shelf. She shook out bits of burned wick and wax shavings from the skirt of her plain day dress. Maggie had grown so fast the past few months that the sleeves of her day dress were becoming much too short. She was now as tall as Martha and nearly as tall as Ethan.

Another thing Martha was strict about—they didn't put on their nicer dresses until the morning work was completed. Maggie was willing to wager that neither Susannah nor Dancy even owned a day dress, let alone one with sleeves that were too short.

In the dooryard, the fire under the iron wash kettle had set the water into a rolling boil. Martha, who was stirring the clothing vigorously with her wash-stick, looked up as Maggie came out. "I'm nearly ready for rinsing, Maggie," she said. "Bring more water."

At the well, Maggie filled two buckets, but she could only carry one at a time. She poured the clean well water into a copper rinse tub which sat on a low table near the fire.

"I wish Ethan were here to do this," she said.

Martha straightened up and pushed at the small of her back with her free hand. "Now since when have you ever seen men doing a woman's work?"

"I don't mean he should do the laundry, but he could at least carry the water before he leaves."

"Your brother was up before daylight carrying water, young lady, but it wasn't for our work, it was for the horses."

Of course, Maggie knew that. She knew he had also split and

stacked much of the wood that was delivered to the house. But somehow that didn't console her.

Martha lifted the hot laundry from the wash pot with the wash-stick and slung the wet clothes into the rinse water. From there, Maggie assisted as each piece was wrung out and spread out across the shrubbery to dry in the sunshine.

It was nearly time for lunch before they were finished with the laundry. If her father could get away, he was usually home for lunch, at which time he assigned her Latin lessons for the afternoon. When Ethan was younger, he attended the nearby Latin School where Cuyler now attended, but Dr. Allerton taught Latin to his daughter at home. The lessons used to be fun and challenging, but recently she'd begun to wonder why she had to continue. It seemed senseless to continue studying every day.

Together Maggie and Martha carried the wash water, then the rinse water, to the edge of the kitchen garden, emptying them on what remained of the plants. "Martha," Maggie said as they carried the kettles back into the kitchen, "have you heard about the revivalists?"

Martha nodded as she stirred up the fire to start the noon meal. "I've heard of them."

"If they're so terrible, why are they allowed to come into the city?" Maggie wanted to know.

"Are they so terrible?"

"They're bumbling backwoodsmen who are in error," Maggie said as she took down the pewter plates from the shelf and set the places at the table. Father enjoyed his noon meal in the kitchen, while supper was served in the dining room. "Why, I hear they've never been educated and don't even write out their sermons."

"And what do you think of these kinds of preachers, Miss Margaret?"

27

Maggie stopped a minute. "What do I think? Well, I don't know since I've not heard them. But I know I wouldn't want to, since they are in error."

"Just remember, people often suspect that of which they are ignorant."

Another one of Martha's sayings. But it failed to answer Maggie's questions and made her almost miffed. "One surely isn't ignorant if it's common knowledge that these people are irreverent enough to hold services in dirty barns or even outdoors," Maggie retorted.

Martha cut up a cabbage and some carrots, added them to a kettle with pieces of pork, and put the pot over the fire to boil. "Holding a service out-of-doors is wrong?"

Maggie stopped what she was doing. "Well, of course it's wrong. We have our churches in which we show reverence to God. Don't you think it's wrong?"

"My opinion doesn't seem to matter here. You're the one with all the questions. And," Martha added, "seemingly the one with all the answers as well."

Maggie felt anger growing against Martha. The feeling was confusing and rather frightening. She'd never been angry with Martha before. Thankfully, Father chose that moment to show up for his noon meal.

Maggie was a trifle worried that Martha would bring up the subject of the revivalists while they ate. She wasn't ready to discuss the subject with her father. But her worry was for nothing since Martha didn't breathe a word of it.

After their meal, Dr. Allerton called Maggie into his study where he outlined her afternoon lessons. Generally, her lesson consisted of copying Scripture into Latin and writing her own compositions in Latin as well. In addition, there was assigned reading in a book from her father's library collection. Today's assignment was no exception.

As her father prepared to leave, Maggie blurted out, "Father, how much longer must I continue to work on daily lessons?"

A look of surprise registered on Dr. Allerton's face. "Why, Maggie, I thought you enjoyed learning. I've attempted to give you the same opportunities as your brothers to expand your mind and to use the talents God has given you."

"But I've been studying much longer than Ethan ever did. He left Latin school when he was only eleven, and here I'm nearly thirteen."

"Ethan continues to learn daily at the countinghouse. Your Uncle Thomas says he's learned not only the accounting but much of the overall management of the entire shipping lines."

"But I'm not Ethan," she answered quickly. Then before she could stop the words, she said, "Susannah doesn't work on lessons every day. Nor does Dancy Truesdale."

Dr. Allerton nodded in a knowing way. "I see. So, tell me, is it your intent to be become like Susannah Clarke?"

Once again that strange sensation of confusion swept over her as it had when she was talking with Martha. It was as though her insides were all jumbled up like the curdled milk in the butter churn. What *did* she want? She wasn't really sure.

When she didn't answer, her father came to her and put his arm around her shoulders. "I propose a solution, Maggie. Your birthday is coming up near Thanksgiving time. I ask that you continue your studies until your birthday, and then we'll discuss the matter. Is that agreeable?"

Her father was always so kind and so fair. How could she argue with him? Part of her almost wanted him to get upset at her. "That's agreeable," she replied. But silently she wished she could throw off the constraints of the tedious lessons that very afternoon.

"Good," he said softly, planting a little kiss on her forehead. "You may work in here, if you'd like. The light is better."

Admittedly, Maggie did love to be in her father's study with the tall windows that looked out on Martha's flower gardens. "Thank you. I will."

"Now set right to work, for you'll be needed to help Martha prepare for our evening guests."

"Guests? Who's coming?"

"I told you the other day that Sam and Judith and the children are invited for supper."

"Oh." Maggie fought to keep the disappointment from her voice. Only the Lankfords. How she wished they could entertain *important* people.

After her father left, she changed out of her day dress and returned to her father's study to work. Sitting at his writing desk, she found herself staring out at the bright fall sunshine and the towering shade trees that were growing crimson and gold.

Actually, she didn't really mind Martha's younger brother, Samuel Lankford, and his wife, Judith. Sam was funny and liked to joke about the fact that he and Maggie were both red-headed. "No one else understands us redheads," he'd say to her with a big smile on his face. "We redheads have to stick together through thick and thin."

She didn't even mind Sam's son, Richard, who was Ethan's age. But the three little boys, Adam, Burke, and Henry, all younger than Cuyler, were regular little mischief makers. And after enjoying high tea at the Clarke home, the Lankfords seemed rather ordinary.

Maggie struggled to collect her thoughts and concentrate on her lessons. Midway into the afternoon, she heard voices at the front entrance to the house. Daytime callers were usually for Martha, but they called at the rear entrance. Who could be coming to the front?

Martha went scurrying past the study on her way to answer the knocking. Curiosity getting the best of her, Maggie replaced her quill in the inkstand and followed. When Martha opened the door, there stood one of the Clarke's footmen, arrayed in his bright green-and-gold livery.

"The Misses Clarke and Truesdale request your presence for an afternoon outing," the footman announced, waving his hand toward the street. At the gate were Susannah and Dancy riding sidesaddle on highbred, prancing mounts.

"I'd love to but. . ." Maggie turned to Martha, who was shaking her head, "I'm working on lessons." The footman gave her a blank stare. Unaccustomed to such formality, Maggie came down the steps to the front stone walk. "No matter," she said, walking past the footman, "I'll tell them myself."

"Maggie," Susannah called out as she approached, "come riding with us. It's a perfectly lovely day. And even though Johnson isn't nearly as much fun as my brothers, we can still have a good time."

"Johnson could even help you saddle up," Dancy added.

Maggie wasn't sure whether to be proud or embarrassed, but she needed no help saddling Amaryllis. Her father had seen to it that she learned to tack her horse the same as Ethan, and she'd never ridden sidesaddle. They didn't even own a sidesaddle.

"Thank you ever so much for thinking of me," she replied, "but I have Latin assignments which must be finished this afternoon."

"Assignments such as school children are given?" Susannah asked.

Maggie flinched. "My father feels very strongly that I should never stop learning," she said in defense. Even as she said it she wished she could toss the lesson in the fire and jump on Amaryllis and ride away with the girls. What a fun afternoon it would be, talking and laughing together as they rode in the brisk autumn air.

"I'm sorry you can't come," Dancy said as she adjusted her forest-green riding cloak about her. "Perhaps another time."

"Let me know in advance so I can get permission from Father." Maggie opened the front gate for Johnson, who had followed her down the walk. He remounted his horse. As he rode a few feet away, Susannah made a silly face at him behind his back, causing both Maggie and Dancy to snicker.

The girls urged their own mounts forward. "I'm not sure I could guarantee advance notice," Susannah said over her shoulder. "Dancy and I are inclined to do things on the spur of the moment."

Maggie had no answer, since her days were spent working alongside Martha doing many of the household chores. She couldn't imagine going for a ride on a whim. "Thanks again for the kind invitation."

The two girls waved as they rode away, their riding cloaks glowing like spring flowers against the dusky fall foliage.

With halting steps, Maggie returned to the house to finish her lessons and help prepare for the evening company.

CHAPTER FOUR

A Splendid Idea

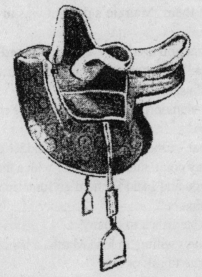

"I've decided I'll cut little pieces of soft flannel and stuff it in my ears," Maggie said to Ethan. She watched as he poured grain for the horses. She knew Martha probably needed her in the kitchen, but she'd escaped for a few minutes before company arrived.

"Are you saying you don't enjoy the chatter of three little

boys?" Ethan asked with a chuckle.

"Four, counting Cuyler. And chatter is hardly the word for the noise they make."

Ethan slapped one of the horses on the flank to make him move over. "Henry's but a toddler," he countered.

"He's learning to chatter quite well and will soon be taught plenty of mischief by both Adam and Burke."

Ethan took the wooden hay fork from its hook on the wall and crawled up the ladder to the loft, pitching down loose hay stored there from the summer. Maggie stepped back to avoid a coating of dust on her clean dress. Their father loved fine horses and kept a stable full of them. Maggie's delight was to assist with the spring colts.

"Take care that you don't say a careless word about the boys around Martha," Ethan warned her. "She dotes upon all her nephews—Richard included."

"Of course I wouldn't do that. That's why I'm talking to you out in the stable."

"Tell you what." Ethan descended the ladder and then leaped from the halfway point, hitting the floor with a thud. "I'll suggest to Father that you and I and Richard go for a ride following supper. How will that be?"

"But there'll be dishes to clean."

"Judith is always willing to lend Martha a hand." He shrugged. "Do you want me to ask or not?"

Maggie wasn't sure what she wanted. What she'd really wanted was to ride with the girls that afternoon, but it wasn't to be. She walked over to Amaryllis and patted the mare's soft nose and felt the warm breath on her hand.

"Are you feeling all right?" Ethan asked.

"I wish people would stop asking me that," she said sharply

and regretted the outburst the moment it came out. "I'm sorry, Ethan. Martha asked me the same thing this very afternoon."

"I can well imagine why. You've been acting differently the past week or so."

"Different how?" Maggie laid her face against Amaryllis's velvety cheek. She knew she sensed strange things going on deep inside her, but she didn't know it showed.

"I can't describe it," Ethan replied. "Sort of dreamy-eyed."

Just then, Martha was calling from the dooryard. The guests had arrived and there was work to be done. Maggie didn't take well to being called "dreamy-eyed," but there was no time to talk it over.

"A houseful of Lankfords" is how Martha described a visit from her younger brother and his family. Maggie could tell from the tone of Martha's voice that she was proud of all of them. Since Martha had never married, she enjoyed doting on Sam's children almost as much as she did the three Allertons.

Martha set a separate smaller table for Cuyler and the younger Lankford boys in the sitting room. After Dr. Allerton returned thanks, Martha sat with the children periodically to keep order, and yet served the others when needed. Maggie was thankful she'd not been asked to sit with the little ones.

Father, at the head of the table, served up generous portions of Martha's delicious boiled beef and cabbage. Sam was placed next to Father, Judith was next to him, and then Maggie. Ethan and Richard sat on the opposite side of the narrow dining room table.

Little Henry sat on his mother's lap to eat but kept hopping down and crawling back up. Maggie scooted her chair away so she wouldn't get in the way. She wondered how Judith would ever eat, but it never seemed to bother her. Judith gave the impression of being the perfect mother, never getting riled or speaking a cross word.

Sam, a lifelong friend of Father's, served as editor of the Boston *News Letter*. Not only did Samuel Lankford know all the latest news, but he loved telling funny stories. Maggie never saw her father laugh much until Sam was around.

That evening, however, conversation turned to the Lankford's church—the Brattle Street Church. "You really ought to come one time to see, Rob," Sam was saying to Father. "The changes in people's lives are truly beyond description. The fervor for God is there, and we see genuine conversions among common folk of the city."

Judith agreed with her husband that indeed new things were happening at their church. Maggie was all ears. Especially when the word fervor came up. Could this have anything to do with the revivalists she'd heard about from Susannah and Dancy?

Maggie glanced at Ethan to gauge his reaction. She'd been meaning to ask him about the subject. Now she wished she had.

Ethan's face told her nothing, and Father had put on his best "physician's face" as Maggie called it. Her father often had to mask his true feelings when tending someone who was seriously ill. Ethan mimicked it perfectly. It was a marvel to Maggie, whose feelings seemed to be spelled out plainly to everyone.

Richard, on the other hand, leaned forward and smiled. Maggie thought he wanted to say something, but he wouldn't interrupt the adult's conversation. As he leaned forward, he must have stretched out his long legs, for a sharp kick on her ankle made Maggie jump. Richard immediately knew he'd kicked her. His legs were getting so long, Maggie wondered if he simply forgot how far they reached.

Their eyes met, and Richard straightened in his chair as his cheeks turned pink. "Pardon me," he mouthed. Maggie nodded, then tried to concentrate once again on what Sam was saying about conversions. What was a conversion? Then she wondered why Richard blushed at having kicked her ankle. She'd known him since they were small children, and he'd never blushed before.

Just as the conversation was growing increasingly interesting, Martha motioned for Maggie to come and help cut and serve the huckleberry pies. Cuyler came tripping out to the kitchen as well, followed closely by seven-year-old Adam, and six-year-old Burke.

"May we have *two* pieces of pie, Martha. May we please?" Cuyler said. His voice all but drowned out the conversation at the dining room table. "We're big enough to eat two, aren't we, fellows?"

"Yes, yes, Aunt Martha," Adam chimed in. "Two pieces."

"I can eat a whole pie," Burke said as he strutted about.

"Go back to your places and clean up your plates, or you won't get even one piece of this pie," Martha warned.

"If we clean up our plates, then may we have two pieces?" Cuyler wanted to know.

"Then may we have two?" Adam echoed.

Martha stood with a spatula dripping lavender-blue juice poised in the air. "The best way to find out is to obey. Get to your places this minute!"

By now, toddler Henry was behind them. As they turned in their hurry to get away from the riled-up Martha, they plowed right into him, knocking him to the floor. He set up a lusty wail, and Judith came to pick him up, cooing to him that he wasn't hurt at all. By the time the pie was served and Maggie was seated once again, the talk about the Brattle Street Church was over.

True to his word, Ethan asked Father if Maggie could join him and Richard in an after-supper ride. Father looked first at Martha, knowing she would need assistance. But before Martha could speak, Judith said, "Oh, let her go. I'll help Martha with the cleaning up. I'm sure Maggie did her share in getting supper ready."

Maggie gave Judith a smile. "Thank you very much. Father? Martha?"

"You have my permission if Martha agrees," her father said.

"Go ahead," Martha said with a wave of her hand. "You missed one ride today. I wouldn't want you to miss out twice."

"Missed a ride?" her father asked. "What ride?"

Martha bustled about, gathering the dirty plates to take to the kitchen. "That pretty young Clarke girl and the Truesdale girl came calling. With a footman, no less."

"Their footman?" said Sam with a twinkle of mischief in his eye. "What's this, young Maggie? Are you getting hoity-toity on us?" He put his fingers in front of his face as though his hand were a fan, waggling it back and forth. "Ta ta," he said.

Maggie felt her face growing warm.

"Now Sam," Judith said, placing her hand on his arm. "Don't be a tease. Margaret can ride with whomever she chooses."

Sam leaned over toward Maggie's father. "Better keep a close watch on her, Rob. The next thing you know, one of those Harvard-bred Clarke boys will be getting sweet on your girl."

Now it was Richard who spoke up. "Father," he said rising quickly to his feet, "that's not fair. Come on, Maggie, Ethan. We're supposed to be taking a ride *before* dark."

As Richard nearly pushed her out of the dining room, she heard Sam call out, "Sorry, Maggie. It was all in jest."

After hurrying to her bedchamber to shed her hoops and grab her hooded cloak, she ran out the back door only to be greeted by

38

Cuyler, Adam, and Burke all chanting, "Maggie's a hoity-toity. Maggie's a hoity-toity."

"Quiet, all of you," she ordered as she lifted her skirts and ran past them. Thankfully, they didn't follow. Perhaps she should have stuffed her ears after all.

When she stepped into the stable, Ethan was starting to tack up Amaryllis. "I'll do that," she snapped.

Ethan stepped back. "Just trying to help."

Maggie's insides were churning, and her eyes burned. She wasn't sure she could talk. "I know. I'll finish."

"Come on, Richard. She can do it herself. When the copper kettle gets steamed up, it's best to clear out of the way." With that, he led his horse out the stable door.

When she was little, Richard and Ethan had delighted in teasing her about her Irish temper. Richard was the one who started calling her a steamed-up copper kettle because of her copper curls. She held her breath, expecting Richard to take up the teasing as well.

Instead, he came over and silently began to lend a hand, not giving her a chance to protest. "Father's accustomed to a houseful of rowdy boys," he said softly. "He's a wit-snapper with all of us, and we think nothing of it. Perhaps he forgets that girls are different."

He snugged up the girth while Maggie fit the bit into Amaryllis's mouth and flipped the bridle over the long soft ears. When they were finished, they led their horses outside. "Here," Richard said, "let me give you a hand up."

Maggie wanted to tell him she'd never needed a hand up and surely didn't need one now. But he was being so kind, she didn't resist. Ethan was fairly well down the lane before they caught up with him. When he heard them cantering up behind him, he took

39

off like a streak. The race was on!

The three rode with wild abandonment almost the entire way to Boston Common. Down tree-lined Tremont Street they galloped, laughing and gasping for breath. The common, filled with evening strollers, forced them to slow their pace as they approached. In spite of the cool evening breeze, Maggie left her hood down where it had fallen during the wild ride. She felt better now, her anger blown away in the wind.

"Let's ride the perimeter," Ethan suggested. "By the time we ride all the way around and take a slow walk home, it'll be nearly dark." The other two agreed by falling in on either side of him, letting the horses lope along gently.

Maggie happened to glance over at the imposing three-story Clarke house on the hill at the far side of the common. "Ethan, do you think Father would consider purchasing a sidesaddle for me?" she asked.

"Our tackroom is full of saddles," her brother answered. "Why would he want to purchase another?" Ethan always seemed to think in terms of money.

"Most all ladies ride sidesaddle," Maggie said. "Perhaps it's high time I did as well. Do you think he would?"

"Why not ask him to give one to you as a gift for your birthday?" Richard suggested.

"What a splendid idea! I'm surprised I didn't think of it myself." For her birthday, surely Father would consider a saddle. She wondered how long it would take to grow accustomed to riding in a different manner. One thing was certain, she'd do very little wild racing sitting sidesaddle.

As they rode along, Maggie's mind went back to the conversation at supper about the Lankford's church. How terrible it would be if Sam convinced her father to attend Brattle Street Church.

What would she do then? Would Susannah and Dancy laugh at her and call her a revivalist?

At that very moment, she looked up to see Susannah strolling with her mother through the formal gardens beside her house. Quickly Maggie lifted the hood of her cloak and pulled it over her head and far past her face. The last thing she wanted was to be seen riding astride her mount without her hoops.

"Are you getting chilly?" Richard asked her.

"Yes, quite. Let's hurry back."

CHAPTER FIVE

The Invitation

One Saturday late in October, Maggie and Martha were busy in the kitchen with the weekly baking. Cuyler had been required to carry armloads of wood until the baking oven was piping hot. While Martha rolled out pie crusts and filled them, Maggie kneaded the bread in the wooden bread tray.

The early morning had been quite cool, but by midday the kitchen was ghastly warm and the back door was left open.

Maggie's sleeves were rolled up, and her forearms were coated with flour.

Having helped get the fires going, Cuyler was then sent to the garden to gather the last of the cucumbers. Martha planned to make pickles after the baking was finished.

Suddenly, an excited Cuyler came running in the back door. "There's a man riding up," he said, "dressed in fancy green-and-yellow livery."

"Oh, my," Maggie said. "That sounds like Susannah Clarke's footman. Is he alone?"

"All alone," Cuyler answered.

"Go to the door and see what he wants," Maggie told him.

"One moment, please," Martha said as she trimmed the last bit of crust from the edge of one of her pies. "*I'll* go to the door."

If Susannah were with the footman, Maggie knew she would die right on the spot.

Cuyler was on Martha's heels as she left the kitchen to go to the front door where the knocker was now sounding. Maggie didn't move. She heard voices, then Cuyler came sprinting back into the kitchen. "It *is* the footman, Maggie! He's asking for you. He's asked for Miss Margaret Allerton. What do you suppose he wants?"

Maggie had no idea. She took a towel and attempted to brush off as much of the flour from her arms and dress as she could. Should she pull her ruffled mobcap from off her curls or leave it? Just then, Martha appeared at the door. "Did Cuyler tell you?"

"Yes, ma'am."

"Then what's detaining you? The gentleman is waiting."

"Martha, I look dreadful," she said. "Simply dreadful."

"My dear Maggie," Martha said gently, "I don't think it will matter to this gentleman how you look. Come now."

Giving a sigh, Maggie followed Martha through the house to the front door. The footman named Johnson stood there with his hat in his hands.

"Good day, Miss Margaret Allerton," he said when Maggie had stepped out onto the front steps. "I've a message from Miss Susannah Clarke."

"Yes?" Maggie said, smoothing the skirt of her day dress.

"Miss Clarke and her mother have retained a dance master who shall be coming to their home on Thursday afternoons precisely at three to give instruction. Both Miss Clarke and Mrs. Clarke request the pleasure of your presence."

"Oh, my! Martha, did you hear? Dance lessons at the Clarkes'!"

"I can hear." Martha stood in the doorway behind her.

"May I? Oh, please, Martha?"

"We must ask your father this evening."

Maggie paused, then turned back to Johnson. "Please tell Miss Clarke and Mrs. Clarke that I thank them for the kind invitation. I'll ask my father this evening for permission and I'll let Miss Clarke know tomorrow at church." She felt pleased that she'd thought of the answer quickly and said it so confidently, in spite of how she looked.

"Very well." He replaced his tricorn hat and added, "I shall give her the message. Good day."

"Good day to you, sir."

Maggie fell against the door as she closed it. "Oh, Martha, I can scarcely breathe. I think I'm going to faint dead away."

"No time for swooning now," Martha quipped. "Wait till the bread's in the oven."

But Martha's practicality couldn't dim Maggie's ecstacy. She twirled round and round as she followed Martha down the long hallway.

Cuyler, who had run back to the kitchen ahead of them, leaped out at her, singing, "Maggie's a hoity-toity. Maggie's a hoity-toity."

Maggie was both startled and angered at his outburst. "Cuyler, how dare you?" she shouted. "Hush this minute."

"We've no time for quarreling," Martha said sternly. "There's too much work to be done. Cuyler, if you can't speak kindly, don't speak at all. Now get yourself back out to that garden. As for you, Maggie, learning not to raise your voice is more important than learning to dance."

"Yes, ma'am." Maggie said meekly. She couldn't remember the last time Martha had reprimanded her. She returned to the bread bowl and punched at the soft, swelling dough, pounding it back down. Anger boiled up inside of her at Cuyler for spoiling her special moment.

"Dancing," Martha said under her breath, shaking her head. She placed three pies on the long-handled ladle, carried it to the oven, and shoved the pies deep into the hot brick cavern. "What's this world coming to, what with young ladies dancing?"

"It's quite proper—really it is," Maggie insisted. "Many families in Boston have a dance master come in." Suddenly she had a frightening thought. "You won't talk Father out of letting me go, will you, Martha?" If Martha ever did such a thing, Maggie knew she could never quite forgive her.

Martha was quiet for a moment. "I've never told your father how to raise you children. I don't plan to start now."

"I'll talk to him privately in his study after supper." Turning the dough out onto the breadboard, Maggie took the large butcher knife and swung it down hard—harder than necessary—to cut off a piece of dough to form a loaf. "Far away from Cuyler!" she added.

Father was late. That happened sometimes when emergencies arose. Supper without father was always lonely for Maggie. She wanted to wait for him, but she knew that was silly since they never knew at what time he would arrive. And besides, Martha was a stickler for having meals on time.

Cuyler had already spoiled her secret by spilling the news to Ethan the moment he arrived home. She felt like strangling him. "If you tell Father before I have a chance to speak to him," she warned, "I'll—"

"Maggie," Martha said sternly. "Empty threats are born in an empty head."

Maggie wanted to sass back, but she bit her lip. During supper, Ethan talked about the goings-on at the shipping yard, all of which was of little interest to Maggie. In her mind, she was rehearsing how she would ask Father about the dance instructions.

Cuyler happily munched on the warm slices of brown bread. Maggie marveled that he should have so few problems.

Following supper, Ethan said he was going out to the stable to oil the tack. Her brother enjoyed the horses almost as much as their father. As soon as the dishes were cleared away, Maggie hurried out to the stable to be with him.

She found him sitting cross-legged on the floor of the tackroom with a harness draped across his lap, rubbing in the linseed oil. Maggie loved the aroma of leather mingled with rich oil. She sat down and watched him for a time. Just being with him seemed to quiet her insides. Ethan was steady and unchanging, while her own emotions were flighty and unpredictable.

"What do you think of the invitation that came for me today?" she asked.

"If it's what you want, I'm very happy for you."

46

"Sometimes when I hear a lively tune, my feet almost take a mind of their own. Now I'll know where to tell them to go." She laughed at her own little joke, and Ethan smiled. "The minuet, the cotillions, and contradances—I'll know each and every one."

Again, Ethan was quiet.

"I'm pleased that you're happy for me," Maggie went on. "But what do you think of it? Of dancing instruction, I mean?" She knew she was fishing about, but she truly wanted to know.

He adjusted the bridle, causing the metal pieces to jingle, then looked over at her. His eyes were gentle, just like Father's. Her own green eyes, she'd been told, were like her mother's. "I guess I'm accustomed to instructions resulting in something more tangible than dance. Don't forget, Maggie, I'm a businessman."

Ethan truly was becoming a man. It scared her sometimes when she saw how mature he was becoming.

"So you see it as frivolous perhaps," she ventured. "But do you see it as wrong?"

He shook his head. "I don't see how I could be the judge of that. You must know that for yourself."

"How do you think I can know?"

"Trust your conscience."

Maggie thought on that for a moment. She wasn't sure she could agree. Could she really trust her own conscience? "What do you think Father will say?" She picked up a piece of hay straw and twisted it around her fingers.

"You'll find out soon enough. Why ask me?"

She shrugged, but she knew the answer. She wanted Ethan to assure her that Father would indeed say yes. Not wanting him to clam up, as he did sometimes, she changed the subject. "Ethan, can *you* trust *your* conscience?"

"Most of the time, I believe I can."

"What does your conscience tell you about the revivalists?"

After some thought, he said, "I don't know enough about the subject to have an opinion."

"You know as much or more than I do."

Ethan looked up from his work. "Which isn't much."

She ignored that remark. "Surely you must feel one way or another about it. Susannah and Dancy say they're unlearned, ignorant men who don't even study or write their sermons. They just jump up and speak with no forethought. I think it sounds just terrible. I don't know why they're even allowed to enter the city."

If she was hoping to egg her brother on, she could have saved her breath, for he remained quiet. Presently, there came the sound of Father's carriage, and Maggie leaped to her feet. "You're saved for now," she told Ethan.

He laughed. "There's never an end to your questions."

Together they ran out to greet Father. "I must talk to you privately in your study," Maggie said almost before he could step down. "Just as soon as you've eaten."

"Sounds important," he said, kissing her cheek.

"I'll see to the horses, Father," Ethan said. "You look tired."

"I appreciate that, Ethan. The Penlows's baby is quite ill. I've been there most of the evening." He put his arm about Maggie's shoulders. "As a matter of fact, I joined the family for supper, so we can have our private conference this very minute if you wish."

Martha must have duly warned Cuyler against saying a word about Maggie's news, for he greeted his father at the kitchen door in a gentlemanly fashion. Maggie sighed with relief. After the doctor had hung up his hat and coat, they went right to his study, where Martha had already lit the lamps.

"This must not be an ominous occasion," he said as he pulled a chair nearer to his writing desk and waved her toward it. "Your face is cheery and all the freckles seem to be glowing at one time."

"It's certainly not ominous. It's wonderful!"

"What could be so wonderful?" Dr. Allerton asked as he sat down at his desk.

Quickly, Maggie explained Johnson's visit and the message from the Clarkes. "It's only one afternoon a week. It wouldn't take much time at all. What do you think, Father? May I go?"

Her father leaned back in his chair and gazed at her. "Dancing instructions. Mm." He rubbed at his chin. "What was Martha's reaction?"

"Martha said she never interfered with how you raised us." Maggie didn't want to tell him that Martha seemed quite negative about the whole thing.

"It's times like these that I wish your mother were here," he said thoughtfully.

Maggie wished the same thing—many times—but she didn't want to talk about Mother just now. She sat quietly waiting. It was best not to try to sway him one way or the other.

"Obviously you're very pleased about the invitation."

"Very pleased. I feel honored to be invited."

At last he said, "I appreciate all the hard work you do alongside Martha each day. One afternoon a week wouldn't hurt." Father stood, came over to her, and took her hand, lifting her to her feet. "I can hardly believe what a lady you've become, Margaret. Yes, tell the Clarkes you accept the invitation. Go on and have a little fun!"

She threw her arms about his neck. "Oh, thank you, Father! Thank you." Her heart felt as though it might explode.

"We have no footman," he said, grinning. "Pray tell, how will you get the message back to the Clarkes?"

"Oh, silly. I'm to talk with Susannah at church tomorrow."
She hurried out to go tell Ethan. At that moment, tomorrow seemed years away, and the following Thursday even longer.

CHAPTER SIX

Aunt Ruth's Problem

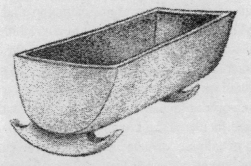

Maggie was grateful that her father was Thomas Foy's step-brother. That relationship meant the Allertons sat in the Foy Pew at North Church. The spacious church with its grand tiers of galleries was the only church she'd ever known. She had warm memories of being snuggled on her mother's lap in church. Somehow, sitting in their special pew on Sunday mornings made her feel closer to Mother.

This particular Sunday, as her family entered the church, Maggie's mind was on other things. Carefully she adjusted her hoops to maneuver down the aisle toward the front. Martha had Cuyler in tow, seeing to it that he behaved. Ethan always sat on one side of Father, and Maggie on the other.

Maggie craned around to see if the Clarkes had arrived, but their pew was still empty, as was the Truesdales'. Gently, she lifted her skirts, arranging the hoops in order to sit down and prevent them flying up. Uncle Thomas and Aunt Ruth came in just then and sat toward the aisle. Aunt Ruth was still wearing her black mourning garb because of the death of her last baby.

Next came the Truesdales with Dancy in the lead. She caught Maggie's eyes, gave a little wave with her fan, and smiled. Maggie nodded and smiled back. Lydia Truesdale was carrying the baby, who was fussing and complaining loudly.

As the bells pealed for the last time, calling to all the latecomers, the Clarkes arrived. Maggie turned to give a little wave and was astonished at what she saw. Pert Clarke and Susannah both wore powdered wigs, the curls of which were piled to a nice height. At the neck in the back hung several loose curls, some of which hung over Susannah's shoulder. Soft tiny feather plumes were arranged fanlike at the crown of curls on top. Their full-skirted satin overdresses swished as they came down the aisle.

Maggie had never seen such luxuriant hair fashion. She was almost too shocked to wave. It was obvious everyone in church was staring at them, but Susannah and Pert seemed to enjoy the attention. From what Martha had told Maggie, Pert and Winston Clarke had been titled people in England and were accustomed to being the center of attention.

Suddenly Maggie felt overwhelmed. She marveled that Susannah would even want to be friends with her. Maggie had one church dress which she wore every Sunday. She would, in fact, have only one dress to wear to the Thursday dance instructions. Maybe she should ask Father if she might purchase fabric to make a new dress. But no, that would never do. She was already planning to ask him for a new saddle. There simply wasn't enough money in the Allerton household for extravagances.

The congregation brought out their psalters as they sang psalms together in lovely harmony. Following the singing, the Reverend Joshua Gee, dressed in flowing robes, ascended the stairs to the pulpit loft. Maggie fidgeted and toyed with her fan, unable to concentrate on the message as her worries gnawed away inside her.

Difficult though it may be, her only choice was to refuse the invitation for the dance instruction. By the time the Reverend Gee had turned the hourglass over several times, Maggie had made her decision. Better not to go at all than to go and make a fool of herself.

For the congregation of North Church, gathering in the churchyard after service was as much a social event as was launching a ship or serving high tea. Clusters of people gathered beneath the sprawling trees to visit about the week's events. As soon as Maggie was out the door and down the steps, she was grabbed by both Susannah and Dancy. Giggling, they drew her away from the crowd and toward the Clarkes' carriage.

"I was so anxious all during service to hear your answer about the dance instructions," Susannah said laughing, "I could barely sit still. It occurred to me to use one of my brothers' slingshots and ping that hourglass, breaking it all to tiny pieces."

"Can't you just see the look on the reverend's face if you did that," Dancy joined in, "with the sand flowing all down the pulpit into little piles below."

In spite of herself, Maggie laughed along with them. How silly to think that breaking the hourglass would change the time or quicken the sermon. Her thoughts of refusing the invitation fled. The girls didn't seem to care what Maggie was wearing. They just wanted her to be a friend.

"Father gave his approval," Maggie told them. "I may attend the dance instructions."

Before the words were out, Susannah and Dancy gave excited squeals.

"You'll be quite impressed with our dance master," Susannah confided when they'd quieted down. "He's just arrived from England and is greatly in demand." She spread her fan and whispered behind it. "But since Mother and Father knew him in London, we have first claim on his time."

"My mother's so pleased to think I'll be growing in the social graces," Dancy put in.

"Isn't it terribly expensive?" Maggie asked, then wished she hadn't mentioned money.

"No matter," Susannah said as though the brush of her fan eliminated the problem. "My mother plans to see to it that quaint old Boston grows in the ways of proper 'societal interchanges' as she calls it. Even if she must do it single-handedly and pay to do it."

Maggie glanced over at Mrs. Clarke, who was talking and laughing with those in the churchyard. Maggie could easily imagine the lady doing almost anything she put her mind to.

"The Thursday instructions may begin with just the three of us, but eventually Mother expects it to grow. One day there may be evening classes with young men in attendance." Susannah leaned nearer to Maggie. "Perchance, Ethan may even want to attend."

Maggie doubted very much that Ethan would ever attend dance instruction, but she didn't want to say so. "You can always invite him and see," she said.

Susannah giggled. "I might just do that," she said.

"Your new hair fashion is stunning," Dancy told Susannah. I must talk to Mother about our having wigs as well."

Susannah touched one of the curls that hung over her shoulder. "This is how ladies are wearing their hair in all the courts of London. My aunt sends Mother sketches—we receive fresh new ideas with nearly every ship arriving from England."

Being with these girls meant that Maggie would be up on all the latest fashions. The very thought made her heart pound in excitement.

Just then, Cuyler came running up. "Father's looking for you, Maggie. It's time to go."

Quickly she bid her friends farewell and joined her family at her father's carriage. As usual, two or three young widows had converged on Father. Different ones continually sought him out to gain his attention. Maggie was secretly pleased that he ignored them all. She wasn't interested in having a stepmother.

As was their custom each Sunday, they drove to Uncle Thomas and Aunt Ruth's home for dinner. The Foys lived just up the hill from the Allertons in the house where Maggie's father had grown up. Father said the house didn't look much different back then, except for all the unique artifacts Uncle Thomas collected from around the world—lush rugs from the Orient, a delicate tea service from India, pink conch shells from the West Indies, and of course, the best pieces of furniture from London. In spite of all the clutter, the house seemed hollow and empty to Maggie.

Since Martha felt she must make her contribution toward the dinner, Father made a stop at their house. Cuyler and Ethan ran inside and brought out several pies to take along.

" 'Twould be ever so much simpler if they would come and eat with us every week," Martha said as they were on their way once again.

"I believe we've discussed this before," Father said in his quiet voice.

He was right. Martha said the same thing nearly every Sunday. Maggie agreed with Martha. She'd much rather have the Foys come to the Allertons' bright, noisy, airy house, than to go to their sad, dark, dreary one.

While the Foys could afford to hire several servants, they retained only a lady named Freegrace, who'd been with the family for years. Actually, a number of servants had come and gone in years past, but Aunt Ruth, who was sometimes difficult to please, was never happy with any of them. She trusted only dear, sweet Freegrace.

As the carriage drew to a halt in the front dooryard, Freegrace hurried out to greet them and help carry in the pies.

In spite of the awful scars on her face and arms from a childhood accident, Freegrace always had a smile. She seemed to shine with an inner peace and beauty.

"The Foys arrived home just ahead of you," Freegrace told them, "and Mister Thomas is putting his horses away. Misses Ruth went to lie down for a time."

Maggie clucked her tongue. "She's still feeling poorly? It's been nearly six months. Do you think she'll recover?"

"Her body would recover were it not being taken down by a sad spirit," Freegrace said as she held open the front door. "She grieved deeply for the loss of the third child. The loss of the fourth was more than she could bear."

"Ethan and I will take the carriage around to the stable," Father said. "You ladies go on."

"I want to come with you,".Cuyler protested.

"Help the ladies with the pies and then come on out," his father suggested.

"Yes, sir." He took two of the pies and sped into the house ahead of all of them.

The windows of the Foy home were cloaked in heavy damask draperies, leaving the house dark and cheerless. Maggie hurried through the hallways to the bright kitchen in the back, where Freegrace would not allow curtains at the windows.

A fat black kettle of brown beans hung over the fire in the massive kitchen fireplace. The rich aroma coming from the bubbling kettle filled the entire house.

Without being told, Maggie went to the parlor closet, took down the pewter plates, and set the table. Presently, Aunt Ruth came out from the front room bedchamber.

"Hello, Maggie. How kind of you to help. Where is everyone?"

"Good afternoon, Aunt Ruth. Father and the boys are at the stable, and Martha is in the kitchen with Freegrace."

"My, my, I really must lend a hand. I can't expect all of you to do my work." Aunt Ruth's mourning dress hung on her thin frame loosely, and her small face seemed even more pale against the harshness of the black.

"No one minds helping, Aunt Ruth," Maggie said gently. "I don't believe there's much left to do."

Aunt Ruth gave a weak smile and moved slowly through to the kitchen. It had never occurred to Maggie before that a person's spirit could be sick inside. But then, she'd heard her father speak of some people who had a will to live and others who did not.

Maggie could remember her aunt in happier days. What an alive, vibrant lady she'd been. How could she be so excited over dance instructions when her aunt was in such deep misery? Surely there must be something someone could do to help poor Aunt Ruth.

CHAPTER SEVEN

The Mystery Girl

The dance master, Mr. Helver, was tall and thin with a hook nose and shaggy brows. His long feet seemed far too big for his body. When Maggie arrived at the Clarke home and she saw him for the first time, she nearly laughed out loud. How could she take seriously a man who looked so funny? She soon learned, however, that Mr. Helver was great fun. If there was anything he could do better than dance, it was make jokes about himself.

"If I can learn how to steer these big boat-feet," he'd say with a chuckle, "surely I can teach you girls where to put your dainty little slippered feet."

Pert Clarke—she encouraged the girls to call her by her first name—played the spinet with a touch as light and cheerful as she herself was. Unlike the cluttered Foy home, the Clarke parlor was set about with the perfect number of appointments and a logical arrangement of furniture pieces. The soft colors were in good taste, lending to the brightness of the large room. The rug had been rolled up and move out of the way, and the place bubbled with music and laughter.

Maggie was sure someone had sprinkled her feet with magic dust. Like a frisky lamb skipping about the meadow, she bobbed and bounced and flounced about, with the music coursing through her. She found herself wishing it would never end.

At half past the hour, Mr. Helver called for a rest period. "You lovely young ladies need no rest, I'm sure," he said, as he caught his breath, "but most assuredly, I do." He seated himself in the overstuffed chair by the bay windows, fanning his face with his white handkerchief.

The girls collapsed, laughing, onto the nearby sofa. "I do too need a rest," Susannah said. "I seem to be quite weak from lack of practice. Mother," she said, turning to Pert, "we may have to have dances every week so I can build up my strength."

Pert laughed. "Every week would be a terrible strain on the servants. They'll need much more training before we hold our first dance."

Hayley came into the room with a tray full of glasses of water for everyone. Maggie found her throat was quite dry.

Pert rose from where she sat at the spinet and pulled a smaller chair close to the sofa.

"Would the servants be prepared by Christmastime?" Susannah asked.

Maggie watched Pert's hands as she reached for a glass of water. They were fine-boned, smooth as ivory, with tapered fingers that seemed especially created for playing music on the spinet. These hands had never been plunged into a tub of washwater and lye soap, that was certain.

Pert took a sip of the water, then thought a moment. "By Christmas? Possibly."

"Then might we hold a Christmas ball?" Susannah asked.

Her mother's face lit up. "Why, Susannah, what a perfectly splendid notion. Why, yes, Christmas would be perfect. We could schedule it shortly after Michael and Oliver return from school for their holiday."

Susannah leaped to her feet and spun about. "How sublime. A ball. We'll have a Christmas ball." She turned to Maggie and Dancy. "Of course you're all invited—and your families, too."

"Come ladies," Mr. Helver said, leaping to his feet like a jack-in-the-box. "If you're to be ready for a Christmas ball, we mustn't waste my valuable time. You're not paying me to sit idly about."

There were several cotillions that Mr. Helver introduced, and at first the sequences were somewhat confusing. It helped that Pert had already taught Susannah several of the steps. After hearing the news of an upcoming ball, Maggie could hardly keep her mind on the instructions. Instead, she envisioned herself dancing about the floor at a real ball. Now she would have to have a new dress.

By the time the hour of instruction was completed, Maggie felt she had conquered most of the steps. Susannah's mother even commented on how quickly she had learned. "You seem to be a natural at dancing, Maggie. How pleased I am that you could come and be with us."

Her words and her friendly smile gave Maggie a warm glow inside.

After Mr. Helver left, Pert sent the girls to the nursery where they enjoyed a grand tea party. This made the day doubly pleasurable.

Later, Maggie couldn't remember how their conversation had turned to the revivalists, but as they were eating sweetcakes and sipping tea, they were once again laughing at the wild antics of these strange people.

"I heard of a mob in New York City," Dancy said, "who followed their preacher through the streets, dancing and shouting and singing. They wave their hands in the air like this." Setting down her teacup, she demonstrated by closing her eyes and waving her arms back and forth above her head, while the other two snickered.

"It's as though they think no one else is a Christian since we don't believe as they do," Susannah was saying.

Maggie wanted to ask just what the revivalists did believe, but she didn't want them to know how ignorant she was about the matter.

"They call themselves the 'New Light,'" Dancy said with a little sniff. "I suppose that makes us the 'Old Light.' How dare they? I don't think conversion is necessary, do you?"

Thankfully, Susannah answered. "Of course not. I was baptized as a baby, and I've been in church all my life, I don't need anyone to tell me whether or not I'm a Christian—I already know."

Maggie agreed with that fact. No one had better try to tell her she wasn't a Christian.

By the time Father stopped by in his carriage to fetch her, she had a much better idea of what the revivalists were all about. And she didn't like them one bit.

A cold wind had whipped up while she was enjoying the warmth and laughter of the Clarke home. Stepping outside, she pulled her cloak tightly about her and put up the hood before allowing Father to assist her into the carriage.

"Your cheeks are pink," he said, "and I don't believe it's from the cold. I trust you had an enjoyable afternoon."

"The afternoon was sublime," she said, echoing Susannah's expression.

"Sublime, was it? That's good to hear. And did you learn to dance?" He clucked at the team and the harnesses gave a delicate jingle as the horses stepped out.

"I did learn, and very well too. Pert said so."

"You mean Mrs. Clarke?"

"She wants us to call her by her first name. It's not improper when the adult requests it, is it?"

"I suppose not."

Dusk was beginning to gather. A tiny smattering of stars had appeared. The air was clear and sharp which meant there was sure to be a hard freeze. Maggie found herself wondering if Martha was able to bring in all the pumpkins and squash and the last turnips. Her conscience was smitten that she'd not been there to help.

The afternoon, however, had been too wonderful to have to think about an old garden. "You should have seen the dance master," she told her father. Her description of Mr. Helver's lanky frame and large feet and the manner in which he told silly jests brought a smile to Father's face.

"Seems to be a jolly fellow," he commented absently.

"Perhaps you'll meet him."

"Not likely. Dancing's not one of my finer talents."

"But if there were a dance, say it was a grand ball, and you were invited, you'd come wouldn't you? Wouldn't you?"

Father looked over at Maggie. "Something tells me this is not an empty question."

"Oh, Father," she said, unable to contain her excitement, "the Clarkes are planning a Christmas ball, and we're all invited. *All* our families, Susannah said. Dancy's family as well. Governor Shirley will no doubt be there too. But," she concluded, dropping her folded hands into her lap, "I would have to have a new frock."

"I see no reason you couldn't make a new frock—you and Martha together."

"But I also wanted to ask you for a sidesaddle for my birthday, and it all seems so very much to ask for. Is it terribly wrong to want two things at the same time?"

At this outburst, Father laughed out loud. She wasn't sure why he was laughing, but it sounded glorious in the still night air.

"My dear Margaret, slow down and back up. You're much too fast for this weary old doctor. What's all this about a sidesaddle? You've said nothing about it before. I had no idea you wanted to ride sidesaddle."

"I didn't when I was still a little girl, Father. But all ladies ride sidesaddle, and well. . ."

"Ah yes, we're back to this subject of your growing up, and I keep forgetting. Tell me, does your sidesaddle have to be a shiny new one right off a ship from London?"

"Oh no." She gave a little laugh at the thought of the Allertons ordering much of anything from London except for her father's medical equipment. "You know me better than that."

"If not, then I believe I can barter for a rather nice sidesaddle. Boston is probably full of them. In fact, I'll start with Uncle Thomas. How will that be?"

Suddenly she felt warm, safe and snug beside her father. She really loved him very much. "That would be. . ."

"Sublime?"

They laughed together. "Sublime," she echoed. "And then I can have the new dress?"

"You can have the new dress."

"And you'll come to the ball?"

"Now, now, let's not get carried away. For the present, let me think about it."

Just as Father turned the team to take the carriage up Hanover Street from Tremont Avenue, a man came running toward them, waving his arms. "Dr. Allerton," he called out. "Dr. Allerton, please come! My sister's dying! Please come!"

"Jump in," Father told him. "Show me the way." Turning to Maggie, he said, "Looks like you'll have to come along."

Father had never forced any of his children to work at his apothecary shop, nor to accompany him on calls. He respected their wishes in their choice of vocation. Ethan had ridden along a few times, but Maggie never had. She couldn't bear to see someone sick and suffering.

The man who jumped into the back of the carriage was of the beggarly type. As he gave directions, Father drove the carriage south of Long Wharf into an area where the buildings were crowded together. The carriage lamps cast eerie shadows on the walls of the old buildings. Here there were no rolling pastures, no leafy shade trees, no elegant flower gardens. Seldom, if ever, had Maggie been down these streets.

Presently, the man instructed Father to turn into a narrow alleyway because, as the man said, "Me sister lives in a room in the rear." Midway through the alleyway, he directed Father to stop. "This here's it. Please wait and I'll let her know I fetched you."

The man jumped to the ground and tapped at the wooden door.

Slowly the door opened and there stood a little girl. Maggie looked, and then looked again. She could hardly believe it. It was the little girl she'd seen on the dock the day of the launch!

CHAPTER EIGHT
Maggie's Best Birthday

As soon as Maggie recognized the girl, she remembered what Susannah had said about her. How Maggie had been warned not to even touch her.

"Maggie, I can't let you stay out here. You understand, don't you?" her father was saying as he stepped down.

Under other circumstances, wild horses couldn't have dragged her into that tiny room that fronted on the filthy alleyway, but her father's expression gave her no choice.

The little girl stared as Maggie followed her father into the cramped, smelly room. In the far corner, lying on a cot with a dirty straw tick, lay a woman whose ashen face told Maggie she might be nearly dead.

Father turned to the little girl and asked a few questions. Her name, she said, was Ann Cradock. The ill woman was her mother, Sarah. The mother had had little to eat since the previous day, and there was no food in the house. The doctor turned around to say something to Sarah's brother, who had directed them there, but he was gone.

"Did you see him leave?" Father asked Maggie. She had not. She was too busy staring at this horrible place. Living in such squalor was unimaginable to her.

"I was going to send him, but. . ." Her father was pulling his leather pouch from his waistcoat pocket. "Maggie, we must There is a grocer's shop over on Water Street at the corner." He dropped a few shillings in her hand. "Take the lantern from the carriage and go purchase cheese, bread, and a little tea."

Fear gripped at Maggie's insides. *Go out on that street? Alone? What was Father thinking of?* Then she looked at the sick lady and the sad little girl.

"The shop may be closed," she told him, straining to steady her voice. "What should I do then?"

"I know the grocer," came Ann's quiet voice from the corner.

"Of course you do," Father said gently. "And he would recognize you. Will you show Maggie the way?"

Ann nodded.

Having the little girl along was some comfort, but not much. Maggie had heard stories of people who'd been beaten, robbed, and left for dead on these backstreets. The cold wind blew down the alleyway as they went outside. Ann's shawl was thin and rag-

67

ged. Carefully, Maggie stepped up on the carriage and lifted out the lantern.

"I've not had a nice light before," Ann said.

"Well, you have one now."

The shop was closed, but Ann knew the way to the back where she knocked and knocked until the grocer's wife came to the door.

"Why, it's little Ann," the lady said in surprise.

Maggie quickly introduced herself, explained the situation, and asked if they could purchase a few items.

The woman shook her head and pursed her lips. "There's no more credit. . ."

"No, no," Maggie said. "*I'm* making the purchase." She rattled the coins in her hand.

"Oh, mercy me, that's much different. Come along."

Maggie waited as the tea, bread, and cheese were packaged, while Ann walked about studying each and every barrel, as well as every counter. From the pennies Maggie received in change, she purchased one piece of candy, then handed it to Ann. The girl's eyes fairly sparkled.

Back at the room, Father had laid a small fire in the fireplace, and water was heating in a kettle. Maggie brewed the tea and then watched as her father helped Sarah Cradock take a few sips from a cup. When he was satisfied that she could swallow nourishment, he prepared to leave, giving Ann specific instructions for her mother's care through the night.

When they were back in the carriage, Maggie's father thanked her for assisting. "This certainly wasn't what I had planned, but that's the way of a doctor's life."

"Father, did you know that Sarah Cradock is not a nice lady?"

"Perhaps not, Maggie, but right now she's a very sick lady,

and that's all that matters."

That night, as Maggie lay warm and cozy in her own feather bed, the entire Allerton house seemed different to her. There were no servants such as the Clarkes had, but she had a father who cared for her and a loving nanny who doted on her. She was warm and dry, and foodstuffs overflowed in both the pantry and the cellar.

Even the next day as she went about her work, Maggie was unable to get the picture of hungry little Ann Cradock out of her mind. In her studies, she'd learned many Scriptures that talked about helping the poor. She mulled over an idea of how she might help Ann.

The following Thursday, after another delightful dance lesson had left them breathless, the girls gathered in the nursery for tea. During a brief lull in the conversation, Maggie told the girls about Ann Cradock, about her dying mother, and her lack of food and warm clothes. "It occurred to me," Maggie said, as she nibbled a slice of lemon cake, "that perhaps we could give her some of our old clothes."

While Maggie expected some reluctance from her friends, nothing could have prepared her for the outburst that came.

Dancy stiffened instantly. "Have some street urchin wear a dress of mine right out there in the marketplace? I should say not! What if someone recognized it?"

"Besides," Susannah joined in, "wherever would such a ragamuffin wear a fine frock of silk and satin? One doesn't put finery on a sow who goes back to wallow in the mud." Susannah set down her teacup and placed her hand softly on Maggie's arm. "Maggie, my dear, I know you mean well, but stop a moment and think— you can't be expected to dress all the beggars in Boston."

"No, I suppose you're right," Maggie agreed. "I guess I spoke too quickly. I had not thought the situation through." How she wished she'd kept her thoughts to herself. What must the girls think of her? But no matter, for soon they were talking of other things such as plans for the upcoming Christmas ball.

As the days passed, excitement of Maggie's upcoming thirteenth birthday crowded out all thoughts of Ann Cradock. And Thanksgiving preparations almost crowded out Maggie's birthday.

Annually, the governor proclaimed a Thursday either late in November or early in December for the colony's giving of thanks, and this year it was to be the last Thursday in November, the twenty-eighth—five days after Maggie's birthday on the twenty-third.

Martha had already set by a good store of spices and molasses as well as a barrel of flour for when the Thanksgiving baking began in earnest. In a wooden cage in the dooryard, a fat chicken and a gobbling turkey were held until time for Martha to lop off their heads and pluck them.

Together Maggie and Martha had shopped for the perfect fabric for Maggie's ball gown, but now there was precious little time to sew on it. "After all the fuss of Thanksgiving is over," Martha promised, "we'll spend every spare moment on your dress."

The Lankfords came for dinner to celebrate Maggie's birthday. Martha had prepared simple fare, since the best of everything was being saved for Thanksgiving—and the Lankfords would be with them for the holiday as well.

Following their meal, Ethan and Richard slipped out of the house and returned from the stable with Maggie's gift of a new sidesaddle. Everyone, even Father, teased her about wanting to sit upon such a contraption, but she rubbed her fingers over the smooth leather, admired the tool work, and was extremely pleased. "Thank you, Father," she said. "I thought you were going to find one that had already been used. This looks brand new."

"Favor was with me," Dr. Allerton said, giving her a teasing wink.

She might never know how her father managed the fine purchase—or exchange—whichever it was. She turned to Ethan and Richard, "Let's go to the stable. I want to try it out."

"One moment, young lady," Martha interrupted. "What about the rest of your gifts?"

"More? There's more?"

Laughter rippled around the table. "Most young ladies would be demanding more," Sam said with a chuckle, "but our Maggie is happy with just an old sidesaddle."

Of course it wasn't "just an old sidesaddle," but as usual Sam was teasing her.

"Here's my gift," Martha said, handing over a small tissue package tied up with embroidery thread. Gently, Maggie pulled off the thread and unrolled the paper. There lay a piece of the most elegant lace she'd ever seen. "Oh, Martha!"

"We'll use it for the ruffled sleeves and the inset of the bodice of your ball gown," Martha said. "How will that be?"

"Perfect," she managed to whisper.

"And look!" Cuyler said, bringing out a bigger parcel from the drawer of the sideboard. "Just look what else. We all got this for you—all of us together." He waved his hand about the table which meant even Sam and Judith had joined in. Maggie marveled that the talkative Cuyler had been able to contain this secret.

The brown package lay lightly in her lap. Her nervous fingers picked at the tight knot in the twine until Richard reached over with his jackknife. "Allow me."

She held the package out, he cut, and the cord fell away. There

71

in the paper lay a pair of soft kid dancing pumps—all in white. The high square heels would make her feel even more like a lady. She could scarcely believe her good fortune. She looked at the smiling faces surrounding her.

Hugging the shoes, she said, "Thank you. All of you. Thank you for your kindness and thoughtfulness." Then she went around the table hugging everyone—except Richard, that is.

Later that evening, she and Richard and Ethan scurried out through the cold night air to the stable. It was too dark and too cold to ride, but she saddled Amaryllis with her new sidesaddle and then mounted and walked her up and down the length of the stable.

Ethan took one of the lanterns and checked each of the stalls, talking softly to each of the horses as he did so. Richard had hung the other lantern on a nail on the wall.

"It'll take some getting used to," she told the boys, "but I like it. I like it very much. This is how a lady is supposed to ride." She came back to Amaryllis's stall and stopped. Richard reached up to help her down.

"Thinking of you dancing the night away at the Clarkes' ball will take some getting used to as well," he said.

"You don't approve of dancing?" she asked.

Ethan stepped up to rejoin them. "I don't think that's what he's getting at, Maggie," her brother said, smiling. To Richard, he said, "I'd most gladly let you go in my place, my friend. I find the whole idea frightfully dull. But Father insists that I go."

"He does?" Maggie said. "I mean, he did? He's told you to go?" Things were moving too quickly. Her mind seemed to be swimming.

Ethan laughed. "Father informed me we're all going, even Martha. He said the whole family was invited and the whole family will go. Can you imagine Cuyler eating up all the refreshments?''

This was turning out to be Maggie's best birthday ever. As much as her father disliked such social gatherings, she realized he was doing all this for her.

It wasn't until later in the evening after all the company had gone home that she was able to think more about Richard's comment. Why wouldn't he want her dancing at the Clarkes—unless he meant he wanted to be there dancing with her. Suddenly her face grew very warm, in spite of the chill in her unheated bedchamber.

Soon they would all move their feather ticks downstairs to be closer to the heat through the worst of the winter. She slipped into her long nightgown and buried herself beneath the warm quilts.

It seemed strange that Richard wished he were attending the ball, and Ethan wished he were not. *Did people always want what they didn't have?* she wondered.

And why should the Allertons be invited to this ball anyway? It made little sense. By a strange twist of fate, her step-grandfather had deeded this fine house to her father and also left him a tidy sum of money. In reality, Maggie was the daughter of an Irish immigrant mother and a hardworking doctor father. Her family was no different than the Lankford family, but they were invited to the ball and the Lankfords were not.

The more she thought about it, the more like an imposter Maggie felt. How confusing life could be.

CHAPTER NINE
The Christmas Ball

The day before Thanksgiving, Maggie went to the market with Martha to pick up a few last-minute items. As yet there hadn't been enough snowfall for the sleigh to be brought out of the carriage house. Maggie hoped they could take the sleigh to the ball. What fun that would be.

The streets around Faneuil Hall and Dock Square were elbow-to-elbow with holiday shoppers. That morning Maggie had helped Martha butcher the chicken and turkey and dress them out. That night the fowls would be put on to boil.

"Let's buy a sugarloaf and a few candies just for the fun of it," Martha was saying. "The little ones will enjoy a special treat."

"So would I," Maggie said with a laugh. "That is, if I can find room for candy after all those pies you've baked."

"We'll make one more stop in here, then we will go to your father's shop to see if he's ready to drive us home."

As she turned to follow Martha into the shop, Maggie spied a small girl dressed in thin rags walking along down the street. She immediately recognized Ann Cradock. Maggie wondered that the girl didn't freeze with only her brown shawl as protection against the raw November wind.

Maggie drew her cloak more tightly about her and hurried into the warmth of the store. By the time they came out again, the girl was nowhere to be seen.

With most of the holiday meal prepared, the Allertons set off Thanksgiving morning for a meeting at the church. Martha and Father had successfully convinced Uncle Thomas and Aunt Ruth to come to the Allerton home for the day. And of course, all the Lankfords would be there.

There were many guests at the church meeting, since family members from out of town were home for the holiday. Fair weather and favorable travel conditions had increased the number greatly. The usual Sunday two-hour sermon was shortened, as the pastor knew the parishioners had mountains of food at home waiting to be consumed.

Two extra members sat in the Clarke pew—Michael and Oliver were home from Harvard for a few days. Maggie had never met the Clarke brothers since they were gone from home much of the time. When not at school, they were usually off traveling. Both looked dapper in their elegant powdered wigs and gold-trimmed greatcoats.

In the churchyard following service, Susannah immediately steered Maggie toward the Clarke brothers. "Maggie, come meet my brothers. This is Michael," she said, indicating the older of the two, "and this is the one who teases me mercilessly, Oliver." The two bore little resemblance, other than their nice smiles. While Michael's face was lean and chiseled, Oliver's was fuller, softer, with blue eyes that laughed in merriment.

"And this is Margaret Allerton, daughter of Dr. Allerton," Susannah said to her brothers, "but we call her Maggie."

Both young men gave jaunty bows upon introduction. "My pleasure, Maggie," said Michael simply. But Oliver held her hand a moment longer than Michael and said, "I understand you will be attending the Christmas ball that Mother is giving. I'd be honored if you held a place for me on your dance card." His blue eyes danced as he spoke.

Maggie swallowed quickly, trying not to choke. "I believe I could find a place. Thank you for asking."

There was no chance for further conversation since it was time to go. At her family's carriage, Ethan leaned over and whispered, "What did the Clarke boys have to say to you?"

She gave him a puzzled look. It wasn't like him to ask such a thing. "If you'd wanted to know, you could have come over and been more sociable yourself," she snapped.

He asked nothing further.

Throughout the rest of the day, Maggie's heart pounded every time she remembered Oliver's words. The excitement of his invitation greatly overshadowed the day of feasting. In fact, she almost looked forward to the day being over and the guests all leaving.

A game of "Button, button, who's got the button," was of little interest to Maggie, but since Ethan and Richard were good sports to play with the little ones, she joined in as well. After several parlor games were played, Judith put her boys down for naps. Maggie seized the moment to head for the stable. Richard and Ethan followed.

"If you ride sidesaddle," Richard warned, "we may race off and leave you."

"Go right ahead," she said coolly, firming the lovely new saddle on Amaryllis's back. "I've ridden alone before. I can do it again." The truth was, she rarely ever rode without a chaperon.

Ethan looked at her over the back of his horse. "That's a fine way to talk to Richard. Are you feeling all right?"

"I believe you asked me that same thing the other day. Of course I feel all right."

"Then why are you acting so oddly? You haven't been yourself all day."

Maggie led Amaryllis out of the stable without answering, chiding herself for wearing her feelings in broad view. She moved to the mounting block which she needed now that she rode with hoops. A jump and a swing up just wouldn't do. She was in the saddle before the boys came out.

"I would have helped you if you'd waited a moment," Richard said. His tone sounded hurt, but Maggie ignored it. She couldn't help how Richard chose to feel.

In spite of Richard's warning, the boys didn't ride off and leave her; rather the three of them sauntered along at a slow gait. Today they chose to ride through the pastures near and around Copp's Hill. They rode along, chatting about small things of little consequence. It was a relief to get out of the stuffy house. The air off the Charles River felt cool and refreshing on Maggie's face.

As they rode down the hill toward the Charlestown Ferry, Richard suddenly recognized someone boarding the ferry. "I believe that's Mr. Leverett down here. He accompanied the Reverend Jonathan Edwards to our church last week. Excuse me, while I go extend to him a greeting."

Maggie waited with Ethan as they watched Richard ride to greet the man, talk a few moments, then ride back to rejoin them. The name Jonathan Edward was one that Maggie had heard often from Susannah and Dancy.

"I fail to understand how you could associate yourself with ones who are in such a spirit of error," Maggie said to Richard as they continued the ride.

"And how do you see it as a spirit of error?" Richard asked.

"Unlearned men who've not been ordained, jumping up to speak before they've even written out thoughtful sermons—of course it's in error."

"How can you pass judgement when you've not even heard what they have to say?"

"The Scriptures instruct us to do things decently and in order," she said stiffly. "I've heard about the disorderly tumults and indecent behavior. Wild people waving their hands and shouting—that's not how church should be conducted."

"When men like Jonathan Edwards and George Whitefield preach, thousands flock to hear them. Can all those people be wrong?"

"It's not difficult to lead weak people astray," Maggie said, which was something Dancy had often remarked. "Revivalists shouldn't be allowed to come into another preacher's area. They're too dangerous."

"Reverend Colman at Brattle Street Church *invites* them to come," Richard said.

Maggie shook her head. "That makes no sense. No sense at all."

"Have you ever seen a life totally changed by the power of God?"

"What do you mean? My life is different from a sinner's because I'm a Christian."

"Have you ever seen a sinner become broken and contrite in humble repentance and then turn suddenly joyful because he knows he's been redeemed?"

Maggie wasn't sure how to answer. The question confused her.

"Perhaps you should come one time and see for yourself, Maggie."

"I never would," she said flatly, closing the conversation. Later she realized that her brother had not said one word during the entire conversation, so she still didn't know how he felt on the issue.

With Thanksgiving out of the way, Maggie and Martha spent every afternoon and evening working on the new dress. True to his word, Father allowed Maggie to decide about the Latin lessons, and she quickly, and with great relief, put an end to them.

The satin frock was turning out more lovely that she'd ever dreamed. Martha could simply glance at a dress and deftly copy the design. Her skills were amazing.

One afternoon as they sat together in the sitting room, it began to snow. Their chairs and the sewing table were arranged close to the blazing fireplace. Unbidden, thoughts of Ann Cradock came to Maggie's mind. She thought of her own warm home, the new dress, and all the blessings she enjoyed. Quite without planning, she told Martha about Ann, describing in detail the sad state of her living conditions.

"I was wondering," Maggie said, "if we might have enough fabric to make a warm cloak for the girl."

Martha smiled. "What a generous, kind thought, Maggie. I believe we have enough in the scrap bag to make the lining. We could purchase a warm wool for the outer layer. Let's make one for the mother as well, since they both seem to be in need."

Maggie wasn't sure about helping a mother who was living in sin, but she'd leave that to Martha. The cloak she stitched would be for little Ann. But even as she made her decision, she wondered how her paltry efforts could ever make a difference.

Several days of snow meant it was time for Ethan to bring out the sleigh, clean it up, and wax the runners. To Maggie's delight, they would ride in the sleigh to the ball.

Martha assisted in creating a crown of copper curls high atop Maggie's head, much like the wig Susannah now wore. They worked on her hair most of the afternoon prior to the ball. Maggie could scarcely calm herself, and bubbles floated about in her tummy most of the day. She had worn her new dance pumps to the last two dance instruction sessions in order to get used to them. They were like wearing a pair of soft gloves.

Martha helped her lace up her whalebone stays till she could scarcely breathe. Her pink shift and quilted petticoat were draped over the pocket hoops, and the soft green brocade overskirt lay over that. The lacy sleeve ruffles hung gracefully from her elbows as she turned about so Martha could make adjustments here and there. At last, she was ready.

Father surprised Maggie by wearing a new maroon greatcoat and new knee breeches with ribboned garters that matched his coat. He bowed low, almost sweeping the floor with his cocked hat, as Maggie descended the stairs.

"My dear Margaret," he said gazing up at her. "You will undoubtedly be the most lovely girl at the ball."

"Thank you, Father," she said taking his arm. "You say that only because I'm yours."

"I say that because it's true," he insisted. "How I wish your mother could see you now."

"What do you think she would say?" Maggie wanted to know.

"Why," he answered with eyes twinkling, "she'd say you'll be the most lovely girl at the ball."

"Oh, Father!"

"I expect you to save the first space on that dance card for me."

"I will," she said, "and that's a promise."

Ethan agreed to drive the sleigh, and it pulled up to the dooryard with bells jingling brightly in the velvety winter night. Everyone was dressed in their finery, and Maggie was quite proud of her little family.

Lights were ablaze in the Clarke home, causing every window to shine golden against the darkness. Even the dormer windows on the third floor shone like miniature lighthouses. Beacon Street and the yard of the Clarke home was filled with sleighs as well as a few carriages that had managed to make it through the snow. Several footmen stood about, seeing to the horses. Since the Allertons had no footman, Ethan would have to periodically come outside and check on the team.

The clogs strapped on Maggie's feet helped to keep her new pumps out of the wet snow. She did her best to keep her skirts lifted as her father helped both her and Martha up the walk to the front door. Even before the butler opened the door to let them in, the lilting melodies greeted them. Tantalizing aromas of cider and eggnog floated about. Boughs of evergreen and yards of lacy ribbons decorated the front hallway, giving it a festive air. The servants had barely taken their wraps when Susannah was there by her side, breathlessly greeting everyone.

"The house is lovely, Miss Susannah," Martha said politely. Maggie wondered if even Martha felt a bit overwhelmed at such excess.

Father also made polite remarks and then was met by Winston Clarke, who was as regal in appearance as the governor himself.

Mr. Clarke shook Father's hand and then ushered him into the ballroom. The double parlors were opened and all the rugs taken up. The furniture was pushed against the walls to give the maximum space for dancing. Refreshments were being served in the Clarke's sitting room down the hall. Here too, the rooms had been festooned with garlands of greenery, highlighted in graceful ribboned bows.

Maggie was surprised to see an orchestra made up of several violins, a cello, a clarinet, and of course, the spinet. Small wonder the music gave off such an exquisite sound.

Surely no court of London ever hosted such a group in such grand style and elegance. The room exploded with a rainbow of color from the men's gold-trimmed greatcoats and ladies' satiny dresses.

Maggie had never received so many compliments in her entire life. One person after another told her how lovely, how "ladylike" she looked. Even Dancy and Susannah, whose dresses had been ordered from London, gave her warm compliments.

After Pert and Winston Clarke had formally opened the ball, others quickly joined them on the dance floor. Just as her father had requested, Maggie gave him the first dance, a cotillion. She was delighted to discover that he knew the steps. Partners changed often and the pace was lively. The white kid dance pumps barely touched the floor, for Maggie fairly floated. While she had thought she might feel out of place, she felt right at home. Dance after dance, fun and laughter, music and more music—Maggie wished it could go on forever.

Cuyler was enamored with so much good food, and Martha was obliged to keep a close eye on him. Thankfully, he'd let his beloved snake free for the winter so that was a worry out of the way. Her father was most obviously enjoying himself, and

Maggie even observed him asking a few of the widows to dance with him.

Ethan, after dancing once with Maggie, was absent much of the time. When asked, he said he was checking on the horses, but Maggie suspected they didn't need to be checked all that much. Whenever he was inside, Susannah was as near to him as she could get.

Many of Boston's finest young men were signed to dance with Maggie, but to her utter amazement, Oliver paid special attention to her throughout the evening. She found herself chatting with him as though she'd known him forever. He regaled her with tales of his travels to India, Spain, and the West Indies.

At one point, he escorted her to the sitting room for a cup of hot spicy cider. Several of the young people were standing about in the sitting room talking as she and Oliver entered—Susannah and Dancy among them.

"Oh, there's Maggie," Dancy said. "Susannah's just learned about a Christmas gift she's getting. Tell her, Susannah."

Maggie and Oliver stepped closer to the group gathered near the refreshment tables. "A gift from whom?" Maggie asked.

"My parents," Susannah said. "Father and Mother just took me into Father's study a few minutes ago to tell me about my Christmas gift from them." Susannah's face beamed as she spoke. "They are getting me a girl of my very own!"

"A girl?" Maggie said. "Oh, you mean your own servant. Like Hayley?"

"Silly." Susannah took her fan from the cord on her wrist and fluttered it about her face. "I mean my own slave. She's on her way now from Trinidad. Her name's Melee, and she's just my age. She'll be perfect. I'm so excited, I can hardly wait till she arrives."

Maggie heard none of the rest of Susannah's words. "You don't mean you'd actually own another person?" she said. Suddenly, all the eyes of the group turned to her, and she felt her cheeks growing hot.

"Why, Maggie, whatever are you saying?" Susannah said. "Nearly every family who is anyone in Boston owns slaves. You know that."

Maggie did know that, but she'd never thought of a young girl being a slave before. In fact, she'd never given much thought to slaves at all. She couldn't explain why this announcement gave her such a feeling of grief deep inside her.

"She's from a very poor country," Susannah explained. "She'll probably receive better food and clothing here than ever before in her life."

"Come, Maggie," Oliver was saying, "they're announcing the final dance. Let's not miss out."

Woodenly, she followed him back to the ballroom.

"You certainly speak your mind," Oliver said as he spun her about the floor. "I take it you don't believe in slavery."

"It seems rather base and cruel," she said, struggling to sort out her thoughts.

"Father never would have owned slaves in England," Oliver told her, "but we had such well-trained servants there. Good servants are hard to come by in New England. Mother plans to begin to purchase slaves and to train them herself. I'm not all that keen on the idea of slaves either, but then I'm not home much anymore."

Whether Oliver approved or disapproved would make little difference to the young girl now sailing toward Massachusetts to become a slave in the Clarke household.

The magical night was over, and Oliver and other of the young men thanked Maggie for her charming company. The flattery was exhilarating, unlike anything she'd ever experienced.

However, on the way home, thoughts of the ball faded and her mind was filled with thoughts of a girl from Trinidad named Melee. Maggie wondered how she would feel if someone took her from home and family and forced her to live in a strange land. How terrible that would be.

CHAPTER TEN

The Embarrassing Accident

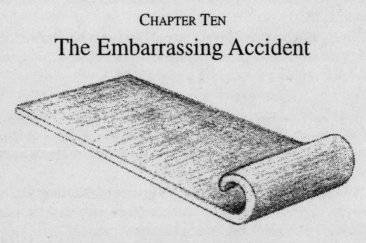

The cloaks for Sarah and Ann were finished the week before Christmas. They were of fawn-colored, tightly woven wool with soft flannel linings.

"Father can deliver these on his next visit to Mrs. Cradock," Maggie said as they folded each cloak neatly. Dr. Allerton had reported that Sarah Cradock was slowly regaining strength.

"Why, Maggie Allerton," Martha protested, "this was all your idea. You should be the one to deliver them. It's not your father's place to do so."

The thought of going back to the dirty room had never occurred to Maggie. She wanted to help in some way, but going back there had not been part of her plan. "We could send Ethan in the sleigh," she ventured.

"Ethan may very well drive the sleigh, but you should be in it."

Martha was right, of course, as she always was, and in the end Maggie reluctantly agreed.

"We can take a loaf of bread, a piece of salt pork, and a few vegetables from the root cellar," Martha suggested. "What do you think?"

"That's a fine idea," Maggie agreed, getting a bit excited. "A little food would be a great blessing to the two of them. I'll go to the cellar, and you prepare the hamper."

In the end, it was Father who took them to the Cradock's. "I have a call to make near there," he told them. "I'll drop you off."

The air was cold enough to form little clouds of vapor as they talked while loading the sleigh in the dooryard. Gray clouds hung low in the sky, threatening more snow.

"I want you to know I think this is a commendable thing you're doing, Maggie," her father told her after they were on their way. "The Lord will bless you for reaching out to another."

"It's not much," she said, still wondering if it had been all that good of an idea.

"What a better world this would be if everyone did just a little," Martha said.

Maggie hadn't thought of it like that before.

Father drove the sleigh down the crooked street and into the narrow alleyway. In the daylight and covered with layers of white powdery snow, the place didn't appear as threatening as the first time Maggie had seen it.

She carried the folded cloaks, and Martha took the hamper. "I'll return for you in about half an hour," Father said as he drove off.

Ann answered their knock at the door with a look of surprise on her face. "You came back," she said to Maggie.

"Yes, I. . .I mean we. . . This is Martha Lankford, Ann. We've brought you some—"

"Christmas gifts," Martha finished the sentence.

"That's right," Maggie agreed. "Christmas gifts."

Ann gave a little squeal. "Mother, did you hear that? Christmas gifts." Ann opened the door wide to let them in and closed it behind them. The room was dim and close. The low fire in the small fireplace was doing little to ward off the cold.

"You may light the candle for our guests, Ann," Mrs. Cradock said from her bed. With some effort she was able to sit up.

Ann ran to get the candle and lit it with a stick from the fire. Meanwhile, Maggie introduced Martha to Mrs. Cradock. The little candle was set on the table, chasing away the late afternoon darkness. It was then that Maggie unfolded the cloaks to show them. She was overwhelmed at the expression of pure joy on Ann's face at the sight of her new cloak.

"For me?" she whispered.

"For you," Maggie said, "with God's blessings." She draped the cloak around the girl's small shoulders, giving her a gentle pat as she did so.

Ann pulled the cloak close about her. She put up the hood, then took it down again, put it up and took it down again. "It's lovely," she whispered. "Thank you so much. I shall never be so cold ever again. Mother, try yours. Please stand up and try on your cloak."

"I believe I'll do just that, Ann." Mrs. Cradock struggled to stand and allowed Martha to place her new cloak about her. Reverently, she caressed the deep folds. "I can't remember when I've ever had anything so nice," she said to them. "It's been many, many years." Tears brimmed in her red-rimmed eyes. "I don't know what to say except a simple thank you."

"We have brought bread as well," Maggie said, emptying out the hamper and placing the foodstuffs on the table. "And a few vegetables."

"We can have a stew for Christmas!" Mrs. Cradock said, taking halting steps from the cot to the table. A new brightness glowed in her eyes.

A tapping on the door signaled Father's return. Ann ran to let him in. "Just look, Dr. Allerton." She whirled about. "Maggie gave me a new cloak."

"That she did, Ann. Merry Christmas! And Mrs. Cradock, how good to see you on your feet."

"The gifts from your household are so appreciated, sir," Mrs. Cradock said.

"The gifts appear to be better medicine than anything I could do as a doctor," Maggie's father said.

As they were preparing to leave, Ann ran to Maggie and gave her a hug. "Thank you, thank you, Maggie." To Maggie's own surprise, she returned the little girl's hug.

As they rode home with sleigh bells ringing, the snow sifted down thickly about them. Maggie settled back in the sleigh, weighted down beneath the heavy lap blankets, content to listen to the swishing of the runners through the snow. She didn't want to talk. Somehow she longed to capture this deep contented sensation and hold it forever.

Maggie and Martha attempted to decorate their dining room as beautifully as the Clarkes' home had been for the ball. It was the day before Christmas, and Father was still out on calls. Colder weather always meant more illnesses, and that kept him away from home more.

"We may not have money for yards and yards of ribbon," Martha was saying, "but we have bits and pieces."

"And plenty of greenery," Maggie added.

Even Cuyler and Ethan joined in the fun. Since Ethan was taller, he could stand on a chair or the sideboard and reach higher. Cuyler cut the boughs and tied them together. The fragrance of pine and cedar floated through the dining room as they worked. Martha had cleaned the parlor, and on Christmas morning all the guests would gather there to exchange gifts.

When the decorating was finished, Martha rewarded them with a piece of her wonderful Marlborough-pudding pie. Maggie decided that Martha must be in a rare mood, since she never allowed this most special pie to be cut until Christmas Day. Maggie savored the tart lemon flavor as they ate together.

Thankfully, Father arrived home in time to eat a piece of the pie as well. They spent the evening in Father's cozy study, reading Scriptures until time for bed.

Christmas morning pulsated with excitement. There were still the usual chores to do and more fires to lay since the parlor and dining room were to be heated. The snow had stopped falling, and bright sunshine sparkled on the fresh white drifts.

Uncle Thomas and Aunt Ruth came loaded with special gifts for everyone. They even brought gifts for the Lankford boys. Soon the house was filled with laughter, happy conversation, and the shouts and giggles of the children.

Although Martha didn't cook nearly as much on Christmas as she did on Thanksgiving, there was still much to eat. *It's more food than the Cradocks will have,* Maggie thought as she surveyed the table.

During the scramble of the gift exchanges, Maggie found herself studying Aunt Ruth. Somehow her aunt appeared less sad. Perhaps it was the cheerful color of her new dress that brought a glow to her cheeks.

Later as they ate, Aunt Ruth joined in the conversation. Even her eyes appeared to be brighter, as though life had come back. Although Maggie was curious, she kept quiet. To ask questions might stir up memories which had finally been settled.

At one point, Aunt Ruth cuddled baby Henry on her lap, talking and cooing to him and smiling. Maggie tried to catch Martha's eye to judge her reaction to this change, but Martha was much too busy tending to the dinner. What with all the other excitement, the matter was soon put out of Maggie's mind.

Richard announced to the younger boys that they would all go sledding after dinner—an announcement that brought forth noisy cheers.

"Marvelous idea, Richard," Uncle Thomas said. "Take them out and let them burn off all their uproarious noise. Why, they sound like a bunch of revivalists at a barn meeting."

Suddenly a quiet hush fell on the table. Maggie wondered if her uncle knew that the Lankfords not only believed in the new revivals but had attended a few of those "barn meetings" as well. Even Father was speechless and looked extremely uncomfortable.

But good old Sam was never at a loss for words. "I must say, Thomas, I have to agree with you. The cries of joy in a revivalist meeting are every bit as spontaneous and genuine as the joy of a little child. And often just as exuberant."

At that point, Martha jumped up to ask who needed what, and the conversation went on from there as though nothing had ever happened.

Maggie felt badly that Uncle Thomas could have been so insen-

91

sitive, but Sam and Judith didn't seem to care what had been said.

"You're going sledding with us, aren't you, Maggie?" Richard had cornered her in the kitchen as she was helping Martha with the cleanup.

"I can't, Richard. Really. . ."

Cuyler, who was standing nearby, echoed the invitation. "Oh yes, Maggie. Please do come with us. It would be ever so much more fun with you along."

Ever since the Christmas ball, Maggie had felt years older, as though the evening had been her graduation into womanhood. Now they were asking her to come and play as a child. She just couldn't.

"Go with them, Maggie girl," Martha encouraged. "Your childhood is fast slipping away. Run off and have fun while you can. Christmas comes but once a year. Enjoy yourself."

Ethan appeared at the kitchen door red-cheeked. He'd been fetching the wooden sleds out of the carriage house. "Come on, gang, what are you waiting for?" Looking at Maggie, he said, "Put your hoops away, Maggie. Let's go have fun!"

What could she say? It did sound like fun. Tripping to her room, she changed into her day dress and left off her hoops. Wrapping her cloak around her and fastening her clogs to her feet, she ran out to join the boys.

"Let's go to the far side of Copp's Hill," Richard said. "The best hills are there."

Ethan and Richard each pulled a sled, with Adam and Burke on one and Cuyler on the other. Maggie squinted from the sun's glare off the snow. Together the little band trudged through the deep snow, laughing and talking until they reached the best hill. Squeals and shouts sounded through the cold, still day as one after another they took turns sliding down, coming to a stop at

Commercial Street near the ferry.

Ethan and Richard raced one another, lying on their stomachs and trying to catch the legs of the one in front. Then the younger boys tried it, upsetting one another and rolling in the snow, squealing with laughter.

Maggie's rides down the hill were tamer than the boys'. She skillfully guided the sled as Ethan had taught her to do when they were younger. She was quite out of breath as she pulled the sled back up the hill after her turn.

"Ride with me," Richard dared her. "I'll show you how fast a sled can truly fly."

"And I'll give you a push off," Ethan said.

Against her better judgment, she sat on the long wooden sled and let Richard climb on behind. With a great thrust, Ethan pushed them to the brink of the hill and let them go.

Maggie had never gone so fast. Her hood was down and the air was whistling past her ears. If they didn't stop at Commercial Street, she was sure they would fly right out over the Charles River—perhaps landing on the other side!

Just as they came sailing down toward the road, a horse-drawn sleigh appeared out of nowhere.

"Look out!" Maggie screamed.

Instantly, Richard turned the runners and the sled veered sharply away from the danger, landing both of them into a deep snowbank.

Maggie had a mouthful of snow and her cloak was thrown over her head. As she slowly sat up and shook the snow from her face and eyes, who did she see in the sleigh, but the elegant Susannah Clarke with both Michael and Oliver out for an afternoon ride. With a little gasp, Susannah exclaimed, "Why, Margaret Allerton. Whatever are you doing? And who is this boy?"

CHAPTER ELEVEN
Consequences

Maggie was completely mortified. How she longed for the ground to open and swallow her up. Thankfully, Ethan had seen the approaching danger, jumped on the other sled, and come down after them.

"Hello, Susannah," Maggie sputtered as Richard helped her to her feet. Clumsily, she attempted to pull her cloak around her plain, soaking-wet, day dress.

In the nick of time, Ethan, leaping from his sled, came over to the Clarke sleigh and jumped up on the running board. "Merry Christmas to you," he said, diverting their attention from Maggie. "Susannah, Michael, Oliver."

"Why, hello, Ethan," Susannah answered, her voice going softer. She pulled one hand from her sable muff and adjusted the hood of her elegant cloak which was also trimmed in sable. "Your sister very nearly got run over. Whatever are you doing out here?"

"You know how brothers can be," he explained. "I insisted she come along to help Richard and me with the younger boys. They are quite a handful you know. And she's such a regular sport, always ready to help. You've not met Richard, I suppose. Richard, let me introduce you to the Clarkes."

Maggie had never heard her brother say so much and say it so fast. He introduced Richard to them, explaining that Richard's father was editor of the *News Letter*. Of course they recognized the name.

"Father does quite a lot of business with that paper," Michael commented. "I say, Oliver, we'd best be on our way. Our guests will think we got lost."

"You're so right." Oliver gave the reins a little shake and the horses stepped out.

"Bye, Maggie." Susannah gave a little wave, then tucked her hand back into the sable muff. "See you on Sunday."

Maggie made an effort to wave back. By now she was shivering and soaked through to the skin.

After the sleigh had pulled away, Maggie turned to Richard. "How could you? How could you put me in such an embarrassing predicament? I've never been so humiliated in my life. Whatever will they think of me now?" She spun around and took off down the road.

"Where are you going?" Ethan asked.

"Home," she answered. "To get warm."

"Does it matter so much what the Clarkes think of you?" Richard called out.

Maggie couldn't answer. It mattered much more than she dared admit.

Late that afternoon, a drier, warmer Maggie said an awkward goodbye to Richard when the Lankfords left. She couldn't bring herself to forgive him for causing her such horrid embarrassment. He did apologize, of course, and she mouthed words of acceptance, but inside she was still angry.

Since Christmas fell on Wednesday, there was to be no dance instruction that week. Then on Sunday, the Clarke family left immediately after church to entertain their out of town company. So Maggie had to wait a full week before she faced Susannah. She prayed that her sledding misadventure would be forgotten in that time. Almost daily, she chided herself for getting talked into doing anything so childish.

Privately, Ethan scolded her for taking her anger out on Richard. "He had no way of knowing the Clarkes would drive along at that moment, Maggie. He felt badly about the whole episode, and you only succeeded in making him feel worse. It's hardly fair."

Maggie knew that. She also knew that Ethan boldly stepped in to talk to Susannah, which he would never have done under other circumstances. Still the hurt wouldn't go away.

The new year of 1744 arrived with little fanfare. On New Year's Day, Father gathered everyone into his study to pray for the forthcoming year and to give specific thanks for all that the Lord had done for them in 1743.

The next day, as Maggie stepped up to the Clarke's front entrance for dance instruction, tight knots formed in her midsection. She tapped the door knocker, and there was Susannah.

"Maggie," she said excitedly. "I knew it would be you, so I told the butler to let me answer. Come in. Come in. It's going to be ever so much fun today. Oliver is still here!"

This was an unexpected development. Maggie had assumed the Clarke boys had returned to school and that she wouldn't have to face Oliver until spring. As the dour-faced butler took her wraps in the front entryway, Maggie could see Oliver coming down the hall toward her.

"Ah, Maggie. There you are. A pleasant turn of events that I should be here to dance with you once again. Michael is tending to business, but I had the afternoon free."

Maggie murmured her thanks as they moved into the parlor where Dancy, Pert, and Mr. Helver were waiting. No one had said anything about the sledding upset or her despicable appearance on Christmas Day. Then Maggie realized that the Clarkes were too well-trained and polite to even mention it. Part of her was thankful, the other part wished they would refer to the event just so she could defend herself.

Dance instruction hour had never been so merry. Oliver's blue eyes twinkled with gaiety as he spun her about to the lilting melodies coming from the spinet. Mr. Helver presented new dances which they walked through slowly before stepping out to the music. If Maggie was confused about other things, she knew one thing for sure—she loved to dance.

At half past the hour, they stopped to rest. As they sat about the parlor enjoying cool glasses of water, Oliver came over to where she was seated on the sofa.

"I didn't know before that you were friends with the Lankfords, Maggie," he said.

So now the conversation would come back to the awful incident. Maggie braced herself for the worst. "My father and Samuel Lankford grew up together," she explained. "They're as close as brothers."

"But are you aware that the Lankfords attend the Brattle Street Church?"

"Not all the Lankfords," she replied.

Oliver paused. "Not all?"

"Martha Lankford lives with us—that's Samuel Lankford's older sister—and she attends North Church with us. You've seen her there."

"I wasn't aware who she was. At any rate, Samuel himself is quite outspoken in support of the revivalists."

"So he is." Maggie couldn't imagine what this subject had to do with her. She knew Sam was not only vocal about the revivals sweeping New England, but he also had written a few editorials about them in his paper.

Reaching over to a small table, Oliver picked up a book and handed it to her. "Since Mr. Lankford is so persuasive and since you happen to be in his company and that of his son's, you may want to read this book by the Reverend Chauncy."

She took the small bound book in her hands, still puzzled.

"This book explains in great detail," Oliver went on, "the evil dangers of the revivalists. They are all charlatans, you see, causing disorder. Quite simply, they are itinerant preachers who jump up and talk with no prepared sermons. It's a frightfully lazy manner of preaching."

Maggie had heard most of this before, and she was amazed at Oliver's concern for her beliefs. "Thank you, Oliver. I appreciate the gift and your thoughtfulness very much. I shall read this from cover to cover." Perhaps this book would answer some of the questions about the revivalists which had plagued her for so long.

"Enough of all this serious talk," Dancy said, jumping to her feet. "Let's get back to dancing."

Following the instruction, Oliver politely excused himself with a low bow. "I've a horse to see about in the stables, so I'll leave you ladies to your teatime."

After Mr. Helver fetched his greatcoat and left and the girls prepared to retire to the nursery, Pert came up to them. "Maggie," she said, "I'd like a few words with you before you go up to tea, if you don't mind."

"Why, I don't mind at all," Maggie answered. She followed Pert back into the parlor, where the woman spread her satin skirts out on the sofa and motioned for Maggie to pull up one of the Windsor chairs.

"Maggie, I've been given to understand you met with an unfortunate mishap on Christmas afternoon. Am I correct?"

So here it came! Maggie could hardly bear to look at Pert's lovely face. Susannah's mother was as perfectly put together as a delicately painted china doll. "Yes, ma'am, that is correct." She toyed with the small book in her hand which Oliver had given her.

"I know you have no mother, Maggie," Pert said softly with no condemnation in her voice, "and perhaps you've not received all the good training you've needed. You're thirteen now, is that right?"

Maggie nodded.

"In two or three years, you will be of marriageable age, and it would behoove you to think now of preparing to be a lady of refinement. The best way to prevent unfortunate instances such as that which occurred on Christmas is to think as a lady rather than as a child. Do you understand?"

"I think so."

Pert tapped her fan to her forehead. "The mind, Maggie. Become a lady first in your mind. Train yourself to think as a lady would in all circumstances."

"Yes, ma'am. I'll try."

Pert reached out to pat Maggie's hand. "I feel certain you will, my dear." She stood and drew Maggie to her feet. "After all," she said, smiling and spreading her fan, "who knows but what someday you may become part of the Clarke family."

An unwelcome blush crept into Maggie's cheeks, and she found she had no words. Pert laughed aloud at Maggie's embarrassment. The laughter tinkled through the air like notes from the spinet. "Go along now. Join the girls and have a delightful tea."

"Yes, ma'am. Thank you, ma'am."

As Maggie turned to go, Pert added, "And please read the book Oliver gave you."

"Oh yes, ma'am. I will."

The girls were all abuzz by the time she entered the nursery.

"There you are, Maggie—at long last," Dancy said. "I thought you would never come. Hurry and sit down. Susannah has a secret to tell, but she refused to tell it before you got here."

Maggie stepped quickly to her chair to sit down, still amazed at the conversation she'd just had with Pert. Her tea had already been poured, and she took a sip, grateful for the uplift it gave her.

Susannah passed the cake basket and waited till Maggie chose a dainty piece with sugary icing. "My secret is that I'm to travel to Salem by stagecoach to visit our friends the Drurys. I'm leaving as soon as the snow thaws enough for the coaches to travel again."

"Why, that's a wonderful secret," Dancy said. "I'm so happy for you."

"But that's not the best part." Susannah leaned forward. "The best part is that the two of you are invited to come along."

Maggie nearly choked on her cake.

"Oh, my," Dancy said with a little gasp, "I've always wanted to go to Salem. What a wonderful surprise to share, Susannah. Thank you. My mother will be overjoyed."

"What about you, Maggie?" Susannah asked. "Will you be able to come with us?"

The thought of expensive coach fare ran through Maggie's mind. "You're so very kind to ask. I would dearly love to go. But I will have to discuss it with Father."

"What do you think he will say?"

"I think he will be very pleased," she answered, but she wasn't at all sure what he would say.

"Be sure to explain that your coach fare will be paid," Susannah said, passing the cakes around one more time.

Maggie gave an inward sigh. Her way would be paid. If that was true, there should be no objection from her father. What an exciting day this had been. "I can tell you his answer Sunday morning at church," she said.

Just then the door opened and in walked the most beautiful dark-skinned girl Maggie had ever seen. She was dressed in a simple printed linen frock covered with a flowing white apron. Over her rich black curls she wore a white ruffled mobcap.

"Melee!" Susannah said sharply, "How many times have I told you not to enter unless you knock." Susannah knocked on the table making a tap, tap, tap. "Knock! Knock at the door first. Or wait until I summon you." Turning to Maggie, she said, "Maggie, this is Melee, my slave girl. My Christmas gift."

The lovely girl gave a little curtsey. "Melee sorry."

Under her breath, Susannah said, "She's really rather addle-pated. I'd hoped for a girl with more intelligence. She knows a little English, but not much. My work is certainly cut out for me."

Maggie looked at the girl again. Her skin was the color of polished mahogany, and her high cheekbones gave her face a look of chiseled distinction. Her slender frame was rather thin, as though she had not eaten well. She stood straight and unbowed, even after the harsh scolding, but her black eyes were filled with great sadness.

Maggie felt sorry for Melee and gave her a sympathetic smile. How terrible it must be to be taken from your family and forced to work for someone else! She couldn't believe that slavery was a good thing, no matter what others might think.

CHAPTER TWELVE
The Journey

The apprehension Maggie felt as she asked permission to go to Salem was as much in fear that Father might say yes as fear that he would say no. In spite of the times she'd spent with the Clarkes and with Dancy, she continued to feel like an interloper —as though she didn't really belong.

The sensation wasn't due to the other girls. On the contrary, Susannah and Dancy had gone out of their way to be kind and thoughtful. And Oliver—well, Oliver had been more than kind. Visions of his blue eyes and kind smile would pop into her mind at the most inopportune times.

To her surprise, her father was agreeable to the trip to Salem and gave his permission for her to go. "I believe it would be a maturing experience for you to travel and meet new people," he said.

"But my clothes," Maggie started to protest. She was sure Dancy and Susannah would take a trunkful of dresses.

"And I don't believe a couple of new dresses would be out of the question," he went on to say. "More of my patients have paid in money this year," he told her. "It's been a good winter."

Maggie wasn't sure what to say. His willingness was a nice surprise. Even Martha took on some of the air of excitement. Cuyler didn't think it was fair at all since he'd always wanted to ride in a stagecoach. Ethan was somewhat noncommittal about the entire thing but did ask if Oliver would be going along.

"Well, of course not," Maggie said quickly. "Oliver is back at school and will be there until the term is over in the spring."

Her brother seemed relieved at this bit of news.

Maggie spent several hours each day reading the book Oliver gave her. The arguments set down in the book seemed sound enough, but strangely it did nothing to quiet the confusion churning about inside her.

When she finished reading it, she offered the book to Ethan to read. "I shouldn't wonder that Oliver would give you such a book," he commented.

"What do you mean?" she asked.

"He's a Harvard man. As I understand it, all the Harvard professors are up in arms about the matter. Frankly, I'm weary of the controversy. I wish it would all die down. Even Uncle Thomas is cynical about the 'awakening' as they call it. If it's all right with you, I'd just as soon not read the book."

The little outburst was quite unlike Ethan, who was usually reserved. But Maggie agreed with him. She wished all the arguments and bickering would just go away.

In the days following, Martha and Maggie were kept busy sewing the gowns for Maggie's upcoming trip. With every passing day, she grew more excited. The subject was on the girls' lips every Thursday afternoon as they enjoyed their grand tea party after instruction time.

Melee's skills at serving were becoming more polished as Susannah worked hard to train her. To Maggie she appeared quite graceful, but Susannah continued to call her "clumsy oaf" and "fumble fingers." Whether or not Melee could understand the words, there was no mistaking Susannah's tone of voice and expression of displeasure. Maggie believed that a touch of kindness would be more effective, but then what did she know about training slaves?

"You should have seen Melee's amazement at the snow," Susannah said with a giggle. "She looked up into the sky, crying 'Magic! Magic!' She thought the snowfall was magic. Isn't that a fright?"

"Perhaps if we'd never seen snow before, we might also think it was magic," Maggie said.

"Perhaps," Susannah said, "but with the intelligence we have, I doubt it. The worst is that she can never get warm. She wants to go about with a blanket wrapped around her. She seems to be cold all the time."

"After living in Trinidad, I don't wonder," Dancy said. "My father says it's balmy there and just like a mild summer all the time, with brilliant-colored flowers everywhere. Too bad she couldn't have come in summer to give her time to grow accustomed to the weather change."

"But she was my Christmas gift, you ninny," countered Susannah. "Christmas doesn't come in the summer." A comment which set them to giggling again.

Maggie would have like to have asked Melee all about her home in Trinidad, but Susannah instructed her friends that they were only to speak to Melee when they had an order to give.

Throughout the frigid days of January, Maggie and Martha paid periodic visits to the Cradock home to check on them. With each visit, they took a few things with them—a blanket or a bit of food—for which Mrs. Cradock and Ann were always extremely grateful. Maggie couldn't explain the wonderful feeling she received from seeing Mrs. Cradock slowly regain her strength. She also couldn't explain why it was one thing she never shared with Dancy and Susannah, even though they had become her close friends.

The trip to Salem was planned for late February. The week before departure, Maggie suggested to Martha that they pay a visit to the Cradocks before she left on her trip. Martha never had to be asked twice.

When Ann answered their tapping on the door of the small alleyway room, Maggie received a stunning shock. There was a smiling, beaming Mrs. Cradock, hard at work scrubbing and cleaning the tiny room. One of the wooden shutters was thrown open, and fresh air filtered in along with the soft winter sunlight.

The straw tick had been emptied and aired and lay waiting for clean straw to be stuffed back inside. Clutter had been picked up and the wooden floor scrubbed.

Mrs. Cradock's face was wreathed in a warm smile as she

came to the door with her hand outstretched. "Welcome, welcome, ladies. Please come in."

"You're so much better," Maggie managed to say. She looked over at Martha. She too was speechless, but she smiled at the sight.

"I am better than you will ever know," Mrs. Cradock said. "Please sit down. She pulled out the crudely made wooden chairs from the small table. Martha set the hamper on the table and sat down.

"Something's happened to you!" Martha smiled as though she had been let in on a big secret.

"My brother took Ann and me to a revival meeting last week. And now I know God loves me and that Jesus died to take away my sins."

There was no denying the change in this lady's countenance, and her voice fairly bubbled over with joy and excitement. Maggie had never seen anything like it.

"We gathered together in a large barn near Roxbury. A barn! Can you imagine? But then, I'm not welcome inside a real church." She touched her hands to her cheeks and laughed aloud. "The place was so crowded there was barely room to stand."

"Who preached the sermon?" Martha asked.

"The Reverend Jonathan Edwards."

"Yes, yes. Reverend Edwards is one of the best," Martha said. Maggie wondered how Martha would know.

"He made the plan of salvation so clear and simple, even a child. . ." Mrs. Cradock stopped and looked at Ann. "Even my little Ann understood. Didn't you, Ann?"

Ann ducked her head as she nodded. Mrs. Cradock stepped to her daughter's side and put her arms around her. "Knowing that God loves us, truly loves us, has changed everything. I feel so clean on the inside, I wanted my place to be clean as well."

"God's love can surely do that," Martha agreed.

Mrs. Cradock went on to tell them that she'd been out inquiring for a place of employment and had been hired by the grocer on the next street. "I want to make a better life for Ann and me."

Throughout the visit, Maggie barely uttered a word. She was too astonished. How could this sinner have favor with God? It made no sense and certainly was different from anything she'd ever heard preached. Later, as she and Martha walked to her father's shop, she asked Martha about it.

"The Scriptures are quite clear, Maggie, that salvation is a gift, free to anyone who believes."

"But Mrs. Cradock has never done anything for the Lord's work. She doesn't even attend church, and she has lived a life of sin."

"We're not born into God's kingdom according to our works, Maggie. One cannot work for a free gift."

Maggie had been in church all her life, and she'd never before thought of salvation as a gift from God. "But what about this Jonathan Edwards—how do you know about him?"

"I've attended his meetings with Sam and the family," Martha replied.

This calm announcement surprised Maggie. Her own nanny. Of course her family never asked what Martha did on her days off, but she could at least have told about such a radical thing as following the revivalists.

The next week was a flurry of excitement as Martha helped Maggie pack her trunk for the trip. The lovely new dresses were folded and laid in the trunk with great care, along with her embroidered bodices and quilted petticoats.

The late February thaw served to open the roads to Salem, and the stagecoach had been running for a week or more. The night before she was to leave, Maggie could hardly sleep. Father was out late on calls and Maggie never liked to fall asleep before he got home. When she heard the carriage drive into the back dooryard, she hurried downstairs to be in the kitchen waiting.

After putting the horses away, Dr. Allerton came through the door. "You're up awfully late. Shouldn't you be getting your rest for the long trip?"

"I'm too excited to sleep."

"I'm afraid I have a bit of bad news for you," her father said as he hung up his greatcoat. "I've been at the Truesdales' this evening, and Dancy has the grippe. She'll not be able to make the trip."

Maggie felt her heart sink. What a disappointment for Dancy. "Does the Clarke family know?" She poured two mugs of cider and she offered him one.

He nodded. "I drove by to inform them before coming home." He took a deep drink of the cider. "It looks as though it will just be you and Susannah and her footman as your chaperon."

"And the girl, Melee."

"Oh yes," Dr. Allerton said dryly, "the little slave girl."

Maggie could tell her father didn't think much more of the situation than she did. But there was nothing anyone could do. She finished her cider, kissed her father goodnight, and went back to her bed. But sleep was a while in coming. She'd never been away from home before. This would be a true adventure.

The Clarkes came for Maggie the next morning in their large carriage, which served to hold the girls' large trunks on the top. Maggie nervously bid farewell to her family, fighting to keep back tears. She didn't want Susannah to think she was reluctant to leave. From there they took the ferry to the Pine Tree Tavern in Charlestown where the girls would board the stagecoach to Salem.

If Maggie was nervous, Melee was even more so. Maggie could sense the girl's fear at yet another change. Melee's cheeks were more sunken than before, causing Maggie to wonder if the girl were being fed properly. The New England winter had obviously been harsh for one who was accustomed to tropical breezes.

A roaring fire blazed in the fireplace of the large common room inside the inn. The tall mahogany clock in the corner chimed seven o'clock. The agent informed them that the coach had arrived and fresh horses were now being harnessed. While Susannah and Melee sat down before the fire and Winston went to the agent's desk to pay the fares, Pert took Maggie aside.

"Don't forget what I told you," Pert said softly. "Remember to think like a lady at all times."

"Yes, ma'am, I will," Maggie promised.

"Keep in mind these are our dear friends up there in Salem, and you'll want to make the best impression possible."

"Yes, ma'am," Maggie repeated. She certainly didn't want to disappoint Pert Clarke.

Just then the agent called out, "The Lightning Stage Line now departing for Salem. All passengers assemble!"

There were only the four of them boarding, for which Maggie was thankful. As Johnson helped her up, the coachman had already mounted his box and was blowing the long brass coach horn. With a loud crack of his leather whip, they were underway. Maggie could hardly contain her excitement!

CHAPTER THIRTEEN
The Never-Ending Party

Unlike the smooth ride in the Clarke carriage, the stagecoach bounced and lurched about over the deeply rutted roadway. The coachman shouted at the team and snapped his whip continually until even Johnson, who was seated beside Maggie, was forced to hang on for dear life. Susannah sat across from Maggie, with Melee by her side.

In spite of the cold air, Maggie was determined to peek out around the rolled-down leather curtains to see everything she could. She enjoyed watching the farmlands and the villages whizzing by. The speed at which they were moving would certainly impress both her brothers.

111

Susannah, on the other hand, had seen these sights many times, and she wanted to talk. She told Maggie about the Drury family at whose home they would lodge.

"Nelda is the older sister," Susannah explained. "She's almost fifteen, but don't expect to talk much to Nelda. Her nose is continually in a book. She's read nearly every book in her father's library. Her mother scolds her to make her come out and enjoy fun and laughter with Julia and me. Julia's thirteen," she said, taking a breath.

"Sometimes we hide her book to get her to dance with us. Of course she can always go find a new one again, but it's great fun to watch her searching high and low for the one we've hidden." Susannah laughed at the happy memories, making Maggie anxious to meet these two sisters.

"Melee!" Susannah said sharply. "Sit up, girl!"

Melee, with her cloak wrapped tightly around her, had laid her head back on the leather cushion of the seat. The girl jumped.

"You should be paying attention to all that I say, Melee, so you'll know what is expected of you in Salem. This girl," Susannah said to Maggie, "is turning out to be no bargain at all. For the high price my father paid, you would think I would get more response out of her."

"But she looks ill," Maggie said. "Melee, do you feel all right?" Maggie started to reach out and feel the girl's forehead, but Susannah grabbed at her wrist.

"Never pamper a slave, Maggie. If you do, they become like spoiled children. If that happens, I will be doing everything for her rather than the other way around."

Susannah's comment made little sense. How could the girl do anything if she were ill all the time? But Maggie kept still. After all, she'd promised Pert she'd not be an embarrassment to them.

Presently, the clear notes sounded from the coachman's brass horn, announcing their arrival at the upcoming stop. Maggie rolled up the leather curtain so she could see better. This tavern was much larger than any she'd seen before, with a wide front porch, an overhanging second story, and large stables out back. The swinging sign hanging from a porch post read: Bogart's Inn. As they drew to a stop, the stable boys ran toward the coach to change out the team of horses.

"Right on time," the coachman boasted as he pulled his gold watch from his vest pocket. "Step smartly now. Lunch will be only fifteen minutes."

Inside the common room, the large table was set with several places. A wooden sign on the wall listed the selections. Johnson took Melee to sit at the far end of the table. They all ordered beef stew and ate quickly, knowing their stay was short. Maggie noticed that Melee barely ate at all.

When they were underway again, Melee stared vacantly out the window. As the coach continued to lurch about, she looked more and more ill. Suddenly Melee gave a little cry, and holding her handkerchief to her face, she threw up right there in the coach.

Johnson fumbled about, attempting to bring a bottle of water from the small hamper Pert had packed for them. Susannah was furious and spouted angry words at Melee.

"Getting angry won't help," Maggie said to Susannah. She took the water from Johnson and wet her own handkerchief to lay on the girl's hot brow.

Johnson willingly scooted over and let Maggie sit across from Melee. "I'm not much good at nursing," he said.

The smells made Maggie's stomach do strange things, but she knew the girl needed help. Melee gave another little groan

113

as Maggie patted the cool cloth on her face. "Sick. Melee be awful sick. Like on ship."

"Pour a little water in one of the cups," Maggie told Johnson. As carefully as she could in the bouncing coach, she was able to give Melee little sips. "You were sick on the ship coming to Boston?" Maggie asked.

"Terrible sick," Melee answered.

"Wouldn't you know it?" Susannah said in disgust. "I have to have a slave who gets seasick on a little coach ride. Such terrible luck I have."

Toward afternoon, the coach pulled to a stop at yet another tavern for a change of horses. Finally, Melee could rest a bit and get cleaned up. The smell, however, permeated the coach, and Susannah continued to complain about it. Throughout the remainder of the journey, Melee seemed to rally some.

They arrived in Salem after dark, but the Brazen Head Inn was alive with lights, carriages, and people milling about. To Maggie's surprise, this entourage was a welcome party for them!

They were met with a noisy volley of greetings and clusters of people crowding about. Maggie had never seen such a jovial group. Laughter and shouts rang out as the trunks were transferred from the stagecoach to the waiting carriages. Introductions were made, and Maggie met Julia, Nelda, their parents, and dozens of other people whose names she would never remember.

The four girls were escorted to the same carriage, and after giving them a hand up, Johnson climbed up to sit with the driver. Melee was escorted to another carriage by one of the Drury's black slaves.

In answer to the sisters' questions, Susannah explained about Dancy falling ill and being unable to come along. Julia and Nelda expressed their sympathy toward Dancy, even though they'd never met her.

Had there been no introductions, Maggie could have told the Drury sisters apart. Although they favored one another with their fair complexion and blue eyes, Julia's eyes were full of mischief, and Nelda's expression was more gentle and quiet. They both sported curled, powdered wigs, piled high with dainty curls.

"Susannah writes to us that your father is a doctor in Boston," Nelda was saying. "I've read a great deal about medicine and find it quite fascinating."

"Since Maggie's around medicine all the time," Julia put in, "she probably doesn't find it fascinating at all."

"Her father has taught her Latin," Susannah told them.

"How interesting," Nelda said, tapping her fan against her cheek. "How I wish my father thought my mind was worth cultivating."

"Oh, Nelda," Julia said, laughing, "Father has opened his entire library to you—of course he values your mind." Turning back to Maggie, she said, "Susannah has told us you have a very handsome older brother. Does he have red hair like yours?"

"Ethan is not a redhead," Susannah answered for Maggie, "and shame on you for telling on me. Ethan's hair is a rich, dark chestnut color."

"If my hair were as pretty a color as yours," Julia said to Maggie, "I would never cover it with a wig!"

And so it went all the way to the Drury home, the girls chattered continually, seeming to accept Maggie, yet never letting her get in a single word.

Maggie had often heard that Salem could boast of many more wealthy ship merchants than Boston. The sight of so many ornate carriages was testimony to that fact. And if the carriages weren't enough, the grand Drury house bore further evidence. This house was every bit as large and grand as the governor's province house in Boston. But in Salem, all along Chestnut Street, rows of houses just as grand as the Drury's lined both sides of the street.

A party was in progress when they arrived, and the house was vibrant with lights and music. Maggie noticed elaborate carvings of eagles and anchors decorating the door lintel as they were escorted through the wide front entryway.

Once they were inside, Nelda turned to Julia. "You go on back and rejoin the party, and I'll show our guests to their rooms."

"Oh, thank you, Nelda," Julia said, appearing quite anxious to return to the fun. To Susannah and Maggie, Julia said, "You'll hurry back down, won't you? It shouldn't take you but a few minutes to freshen up and change."

Come back down? Maggie could hardly believe it. All she wanted was to crawl into bed. But she was soon to learn that the society of Salem held parties late and slept till noon. As they followed Nelda up the stairs, Maggie asked Susannah about Melee's whereabouts.

"Now Maggie, don't you worry about that girl. Johnson has taken her to the slaves' quarters down in the basement. She'll be fine."

"You have your own slave girl now, Susannah?" At the top of the stairs, Nelda turned to lead them down a long hallway.

"She's a Christmas gift from my parents."

"Don't you find it is a great deal of work to train them? Mother spends hours trying to train our slaves properly. Sometimes I wonder if it's worth it all." She stopped and opened the door of a large bedchamber where a good fire had been laid in the fireplace. It looked cozy and inviting.

"We gave you this room, Maggie, and Susannah will be right across the hall. I hope you'll be comfortable. If you need anything, simply use the bellpull there by the draperies."

Maggie's trunk had arrived ahead of her and sat open at the foot of the tall cherrywood bed.

"Thank you very much. I know I shall be very comfortable."

"Put on one of your party dresses," Susannah told her. "I'll see you in a few minutes."

The party lasted until the wee hours of the morning. Every time Maggie tried to sit out a dance, either Julia or Susannah pulled her back in again. Never could she have imagined not wanting to dance, but she'd slept very little the night before and was exhausted. By the time she did climb the stairs to her room, she could barely hold her eyes open long enough to get out of her dress and into her nightgown.

As she settled into the high, soft bed, her thoughts turned to Melee. No matter what Susannah said, Maggie's heart went out to the girl. *Why,* she wondered, *does there have to be such a terrible thing as slavery?*

When Maggie awakened the next morning, it was broad daylight. The last time she'd slept this late, it was because she was ill. Having no idea what she should do, she arose and dressed. No one told her when breakfast would be served. She looked at the bellpull. At least she could ask one of the servants. Cautiously, she tugged at the tasseled pull.

Presently a tap sounded at the door. She opened to see one of the uniformed slaves neatly dressed in a dark bodice and skirt, with starched white collar and apron. A ribboned mobcap with long ruffles in back covered her dark hair.

"Morning, m'lady," she said. "My name's Bessie. You is up mighty early."

"Early?" She glanced at the sun streaming in the windows. "Why, it must be nearly noon."

117

"Most folks in this house don't get up 'fore noon, m'lady. Less it's them menfolk going on a hunt. But that don't happen till weather warms. Shall I bring breakfast?"

"Is breakfast being served downstairs?" Maggie would much rather eat with someone.

The girl shook her head. "They take breakfast in they rooms, then come down for lunch," Bessie explained.

"Very well, Bessie." Maggie was too hungry to object. "Please bring my breakfast." She felt silly ordering this girl about, and she'd never been called "my lady" in her life.

When the tray arrived, she ate at a small table by the window overlooking the formal gardens. There were fountains, stone benches, and tall well-manicured shrubs. The outlines of flower beds showed promise of an explosion of color when spring fully arrived.

She quickly devoured the light milk biscuits and pieces of salty ham, washing it down with cups of hot tea. But when she'd finished eating, she had nothing to do. Another full hour dragged by before Susannah knocked at her door, urging her to come down for lunch.

Many of those who had been at the dance the night before were overnight guests as well, so the lunch table was large and spread with a fare as fine as Martha's Thanksgiving dinner.

That afternoon Mrs. Drury accompanied the girls in the carriage to the shops in Salem. Maggie had never in her life seen so many pretty and expensive things. The number of fine shops far outnumbered those in Boston, and the women seemed intent on taking in every one.

Susannah, of course, had money with her and made several purchases. Maggie had just a little money her father had given her, but she'd planned to purchase gifts for her family members. So while the others were buying for themselves, she searched for the needed gift items.

Upon their return home, the ladies were served a light tea and then encouraged to rest in their rooms before the frolic which was scheduled for that evening.

In Maggie's world, a frolic referred to quilting bees or apple paring time when groups of people gathered to work together. In the world of the Drury family, a frolic simply meant traveling from one home to the next, or sometimes to a large tavern, where the young people gathered for games, dancing, and refreshments.

Maggie soon learned that activities had been planned for nearly every evening of their two-week stay. The afternoons were filled with needlework and reading, but occasionally there were activities in the afternoon as well. Maggie asked Nelda for permission to borrow books from the library, since she continually awakened before the others of the household. Kindly, Nelda led her to the library and allowed her to make her own choices.

Before the first week was out, Maggie was plagued with an intense case of homesickness. Everything here seemed frivolous and meaningless. Even the Sabbath was taken less seriously than in Boston. Other than snippets of men's conversation regarding business, most of the conversation was empty and hollow. She recalled how she could talk to Ethan about most anything—especially things of a serious nature. She missed him terribly. She even missed the Latin assignments she'd been so happy to end after her birthday.

Her hands ached for something substantial to do. If she'd seen the servants doing laundry, she would have pushed them aside and started wringing clothes out herself! But of course she never saw them doing any work. The house was so large, all the laundry was done in the basement, and the kitchens were at the far end of the lower floor.

She caught quick glimpses of Melee as the slave girl went in and out of Susannah's room, waiting on her mistress. In spite of the girl's dark skin coloring, she appeared sallow and ashen. Maggie was more concerned for her than ever.

Two nights before they were to leave, Maggie was in her room preparing for bed. The Drury home was like a wayside inn with guests coming and going continually. That afternoon they had ridden in carriages to Crowinshield's Wharf to meet a new set of friends arriving from London. That evening there was yet another party held in Susannah and Maggie's honor.

Maggie was thoroughly exhausted. Sitting on the chair by the windows, she pulled off her dance pumps and studied them, fully expecting to see holes worn in the soles from so much dancing. Suddenly, movement in the garden below caught her attention. She pushed open the window to get a better look. There on one of the stone benches sat a small, hunched form. In the dim soft moonlight Maggie could barely see, but she was certain the form was Melee!

CHAPTER FOURTEEN

Maggie Dares to Help

There was only one way for Maggie to find out for sure who was huddled all alone in the garden. She pulled her wrapper about her, grabbed her cloak, and ran down the stairs. Winding through a maze of hallways, she searched for the back entrance. When she found it, it took a few minutes for her to get her bearings from where she saw the figure.'While the March night air wasn't as frigid as winter, it was still very cold. Weaving in and out through the tall shrubberies, she drew her cloak more tightly around her.

At last, she followed around a curving path and there on the bench sat the weeping, trembling Melee.

"Melee, whatever are you doing out here? You'll freeze."

Melee looked up and drew back with fear in her eyes. "Sorry. Melee sorry."

"Sorry for what? You haven't done anything." Maggie sat down on the cold bench beside her. "Why are you out here? Don't you have a room and a bed?"

"They laugh at Melee."

"Who laughs?"

"House people."

"The servants?"

Melee nodded. "Other slaves laugh."

"Sometimes people make fun of what they don't understand, Melee." She remembered how Martha had said that to her once. Since most of the Drury slaves were from Africa, could they have made fun of her speech? Perhaps her appearance? Who knew?

"Don't listen to them, Melee." Not sure how much Melee actually understood, Maggie put her hands over her ears. "Ignore them. Pretend you don't hear. Now you need to get back inside and get to bed."

Melee's thin body convulsed in a hard shiver. "Lock door," she said.

"Who locked the door? What door?"

Melee shrugged.

"The room where you sleep? Is that the door which is locked?" She nodded.

"Poor girl," Maggie said, gently putting her arm around her. It was then she realized Melee was not shivering from cold. She had a fever and was shaking from chills. That settled it! She helped Melee to her feet. "You're coming with me," Maggie told her.

Not bothering to attempt to find the servants' entrance, she led Melee along the paths. Making her way slowly to the door, she helped Melee inside and then up to her room where the fire was still banked and warm. With a bit of effort, Maggie assisted the girl up the steps into the high bed and tucked her in.

She dampened a cloth in the water pitcher and laid it across Melee's forehead. "I'm sure Massachusetts is nothing like Trinidad," she said softly. "How difficult all this must be for you."

"Trinidad." Melee's eyes fluttered open in response to the word. "Flowers," she said weakly. "Pretty flowers. Much sunshine. Mama, Papa."

"Poor girl," Maggie said, patting her shoulder. Nourishment was what she needed, and soon. Maggie stepped to the window and tugged at the tasseled bellpull. Within minutes Bessie was at the door, sleepy-eyed and dressed in a white wrapper.

"Bessie, I need your help." Maggie drew her inside and waved to the bed. "This girl is very sick. I need warm milk, a bowl of gruel, and perhaps a few stewed quince. Can you do that for me?"

"What girl be sick?" Bessie asked. "Misses Drury should be told."

"No, no. Don't tell anyone. I have Melee here."

Suddenly Bessie's eyes flew open. "You have the slave girl in your bed? Oh my! Oh my!"

With that, she was out the door and across the hall banging on the door and shouting, "Miss Susannah, Miss Susannah, come quick. Come see. The Miss Margaret done put a slave in her bed! In her *bed!*"

One door opened in the hallway, then another and another. Questions were whispered. Slippered feet shuffled. Presently Susannah was standing incredulous in the room, followed quickly by Nelda, Julia, and their parents.

"Maggie," Susannah demanded, "what's the meaning of this? Why is this girl in your own bed?"

Maggie's fear of what Susannah might think had vanished. "She's sick. She was locked out of her room by the others in the basement quarters. She has fever, and she would have died in the night air. I had no choice but to bring her in."

"You had no right. She's my slave. You should have brought her to me."

"Perhaps I should have. But I didn't."

"Please," Mrs. Drury interrupted, "let there be no anger." Turning to Susannah, she said, "Didn't you tell me Maggie has no servants or slaves? So how could she possibly know the right way to handle the situation?"

The condescending tone infuriated Maggie further. "I would never own a slave," she snapped. "But if I did, I'd know enough to extend help when one is suffering."

Mrs. Drury smiled and ignored the outburst as though Maggie were a child throwing a tantrum. "Bessie."

"Yes m'lady?"

"Fetch Susannah's footman. Have him come and take this girl back to her quarters. Then you stay with her tonight."

Bessie rolled her eyes. "Yes m'lady."

The crowd in the hallway was still buzzing when Mr. Drury ordered everyone back to bed. "Just a simple mistake," he told them. "Nothing to get upset about."

As Susannah turned to go, she whispered to Maggie, "Wait till Mother learns how terribly you behaved and how you embarrassed me before all my friends."

"I was not thinking of you," Maggie stated flatly, "but of the girl."

After Melee had been carried away by Johnson, Mrs. Drury

ordered the linens to be completely stripped from the bed and fresh ones put on before Maggie could retire for the night. By the time all the commotion had quieted down, Maggie was still fuming. The copper kettle was definitely steamed up.

The remaining two days in Salem were rather awkward. Guests looked at Maggie with mirthful eyes and twittered behind spread silk fans. The Drurys now spoke to her in patronizing tones, but Maggie had ceased to care. She no longer ached to please Susannah or to "think like a lady" according to Pert's orders.

Her attempts to learn of Melee's condition were ignored. Had there been more than two days before departure, she would have searched for the servants' quarters and banged on every door until she found the sick slave girl.

As the carriages were being loaded before dawn on Saturday morning, Johnson came from the rear of the house, carrying Melee. Maggie was relieved to see that the girl's dark eyes were brighter, but she was still too weak to walk.

The journey home was punctuated by Susannah's complaints about having sick slave girl. At last, Maggie could bear no more. "If you were to take care of her properly," she said, "Melee would not only be well and healthy, she would be more pleased to serve you."

"You know nothing about owning a slave," Susannah retorted with a little sniff.

"Owning another person is wrong," Maggie stated. She was surprised at her own brashness, but once the words were out she felt good. For once she'd spoken what she truly believed.

"I didn't *make* Melee a slave," Susannah shot back. "She was already a slave. We simply made a purchase. If you're so against slaves, why don't you talk to your Uncle Thomas? Melee came in on one of his ships."

Maggie didn't answer because she knew Susannah was right. But her comment gave Maggie an idea.

That evening they were met in Cambridge by Pert and several footmen in one of the Clarkes' carriages. Susannah wasted no time in relating the incident with Melee in vivid detail. Pert reacted to the incident exactly as Mrs. Drury had—attributing Maggie's action to simple ignorance.

"Maggie still has a great deal to learn," Pert said to Susannah as though Maggie were not sitting right there in the carriage with them.

Maggie gave a polite smile and let the comment pass. How relieved she was when they drove up to the Allerton house and all her family was there to greet her. Cuyler bounced around everywhere, excited to see if Maggie brought him a gift. Even Ethan gave her a warm hug of welcome.

Once her things were unloaded and the Clarkes were gone, she was treated to some of Martha's wonderful plain cooking. How she'd missed it in the endless array of rich dainties at the Drurys's!

As they gathered about to hear all her stories, she told them of Melee's illness—carefully omitting the part about Melee in her bed. "Can you attend to her, Father? She needs help desperately."

"I understand your concern, Maggie, but I can't go unless they call me."

Maggie shook her head. "I'm not sure they will."

"But we can pray for her," Martha said.

"Of course," Maggie agreed. *Why hadn't she thought of prayer?*

They bowed their heads, and Father led the prayer, asking for Melee's safety and well-being.

As they ate, Maggie surprised her father by asking him to reinstate her Latin lessons. When he asked her what prompted the decision, she simply said, "I now appreciate the fact that you think my mind is worth cultivating."

When their meal was finished, Maggie turned to her brother and said, "Ethan, let's go for a ride."

Ethan jumped up from the table. "I was hoping you'd say that."

"Father, may we ride over and see Uncle Thomas? I've something to ask him."

"Why, of course. There's no need to ask permission to see your own uncle."

"I may not be invited back to the Clarkes for dance instruction," Maggie told Ethan as they trotted out over the pastures toward the Foy home.

"You don't sound too upset. A few months ago you were captivated by the Clarkes. Did something happen on your trip?"

"Many things happened. But most of it happened on the inside of me. I see things differently now. On Christmas Day, I told Richard that it mattered to me what the Clarkes thought of me, but that's not true anymore." When she told him of finding the sick Melee and putting her in her own bed, Ethan laughed right out loud.

"How I wish I'd been there," he said. "What a sight to see the shock on their faces. I'm proud of you, Maggie. Very proud of you."

Maggie hadn't thought of Ethan being proud of her actions. She only wanted to help Melee. But it was nice to have his approval. Later, she would tell Father and Martha as well.

"I must warn you about something before we get to Uncle Thomas's," Ethan said, changing the subject.

Maggie turned to look at his face. "Aunt Ruth's not taken a turn for the worse, has she? She looked so much better on Christmas Day."

"Quite the opposite. She's totally changed."

"Changed how?" she asked as they rode into the Foys' back dooryard.

"You'll have to see for yourself. I'll only tell you that she calls it a conversion."

"Conversion?"

"She went to one of the meetings that Richard is always talking about and she says. . ." He dismounted and came around to help her down. "I'll not say anymore. I'll let her tell you."

Ethan was right—not only was there a change in Aunt Ruth, but in the entire house. The dark heavy draperies were gone. The house was bright and airy. Freegrace was beaming, and Aunt Ruth looked years younger. The change in Aunt Ruth was similar to what Maggie had seen in Mrs. Cradock. Perhaps Richard and Sam Lankford were right—perhaps there was something to this "awakening" after all.

Ethan and Maggie were ushered into the parlor, as Aunt Ruth asked several questions about Maggie's trip. Maggie politely answered them all, then said, "I'd like to talk to Uncle Thomas about something that occurred on my trip, but first, Aunt Ruth, please tell me what's happened to you."

By now Uncle Thomas had come in from his study. Quietly he removed his spectacles, folded them into their case, and sat down on the sofa beside his wife and took her hand.

"I'm not sure how to explain it, Maggie," Aunt Ruth began. "I thought I was a Christian because I attended church, but as I attended the revivalist meetings, my heart was softened and touched. I wept for hours. Not tears of grief like for our babies, but of repentance. Tears of genuine sorrow for my sins."

As Aunt Ruth talked, Freegrace served tea, smiling and nodding as she listened.

"But you're not a sinner," Maggie protested. "You have never done anything wrong. You have always done good things for others."

"The Scriptures tell us that all of us have fallen and come short of the glory of God, Maggie. That's why Jesus died for us—to pay for our sins. It's not according to our works, but rather by His gift."

Maggie recalled the day Martha had told her that very same thing, that salvation was a gift for all.

"I simply made the decision to open my heart and let Him in," Aunt Ruth continued. "When I did, He cleansed away all the pain and grief, and I was flooded with peace and joy."

Maggie looked at Ethan and could tell he was touched by their aunt's words.

"She could go on and on," Uncle Thomas interrupted, "and sometimes she does. But I heard you say you wanted to talk to me about a matter. What is it?"

Maggie knew they must get home before dark, so she needed to get to the point. Quickly she explained about Melee and her mistreatment by Susannah.

"I've come to ask you to purchase Melee, set her free, and send her back home. I know it would cost a great deal, but the girl is quite ill and extremely homesick. Why, just being away from my family for a fortnight was almost unbearable for me. What a nightmare it would be to be sent away from them forever!"

Uncle Thomas had listened closely. Now he leaned back in the sofa and shook his head. "I'm sorry, Maggie. I understand your feelings, and I admire your mercy. Would that all persons had your measure of love and compassion. But Winston Clarke would never sell that girl to me."

"But she came to Boston on your ship," Maggie said, hoping

to persuade him further.

"I'm not personally involved in any slave trade, Maggie. I admit that I have transported slaves on my ships, but I've always done it for others who are involved in the market."

"Perhaps we should consider putting a stop to our limited involvement, Thomas," Aunt Ruth said softly. "Maggie is making me rethink my feelings about this matter of buying and selling another person."

"You may be right," Uncle Thomas said to her. To Maggie he said, "I wish I could grant your request, but Winston Clarke is a hardheaded competitor of mine and a tough-minded businesman. That girl is his property, and he would never agree to sell her."

"You can ask the Lord to take care of her, Maggie," Aunt Ruth suggested.

"Martha suggested that very thing," Maggie said, "and we all prayed together as a family."

"Then you must rest in the fact that God will hear and answer your prayer."

Maggie wasn't sure. The best thing for Melee was to be able to go home. And Maggie wanted desperately to help her get there.

Chapter Fifteen
Free at Last

The remainder of March turned blustery and sharply colder.

Gray day followed upon gray day, and spring appeared to be delayed indefinitely.

To Maggie's surprise, she was indeed invited to return to Thursday dance instruction, but the joy had gone out of it. When she learned that Melee was bedfast and when Susannah continued to complain about having a sick slave, Maggie found she could no longer bear to be there. How could she laugh and dance when Melee lay ill? Even Dancy seemed somewhat subdued.

Late one night, Maggie had been in bed only a short time when she heard a commotion at the back door. She thought little of it since people often sent messengers at all hours to fetch her doctor father.

Presently, however, her father was knocking at the door of her bedchamber. "Maggie," he said, "I've been summoned to go tend the Clarkes' slave girl."

Maggie flew out of her bed, pulling her wrapper about her. Opening the door, she said, "Oh, Father, thank heaven. God has surely answered our prayers."

"Knowing your deep concern for her, I've come to ask you to accompany me."

"Me go with you?" She was stunned. Her father had never asked such a thing. "Why, yes, I would like that. Thank you."

"I'll harness the horses. Come as soon as you can."

Maggie was dressed and outside in no time. As they rode to the Clarke home in silence, Maggie continued to pray for Melee.

Winston Clarke was the one who directed them to the rear of the house where the servants' quarters were located. Maggie wasn't sure if Susannah or Pert were even aware that Dr. Allerton had been called. Neither of them came out.

They found Melee lying on a small cot in a corner of the servants' kitchen. It was warm and clean there, but she was so alone. The girls' dark eyes brightened at the sight of Maggie.

"Maggie," she whispered. "Maggie is friend."

Tears burned in Maggie's eyes. This girl desperately needed a friend, and Maggie had been fortunate to be that friend. She waited as her father examined Melee. A solemn Winston Clarke stood nearby. Presently, Father approached Mr. Clarke.

"She's very ill," Maggie's father said. "I would ask your permission to allow us to take Melee to our home where I can give her closer attention."

Maggie couldn't have been more shocked! In all her days, she'd never heard her father ask to take a patient to their home. A few had slept over in the upstairs rooms at his apothecary shop, but never in their home. Maggie held her breath, waiting for Mr. Clarke's answer.

"Do you think you can save her life?" Winston asked. "She's worth a great deal of money."

"If she's in my total care, perhaps. Without it, she may not live to see another week."

"As you think best. Your carriage is open, is it not?"

Father nodded. "It is."

"Then I'll order one of our carriages to transport her immediately."

"Very good," Father replied. "Maggie, you ride with Melee."

And so it was that before the night was out, Melee was bedded down safely in the Allerton home, surrounded by love and attention. Martha doted over the girl as though she were one of the family, and even Cuyler wanted to help by fetching whatever was needed.

Maggie was never sure how the Lankfords got word of the situation, but the next evening, Richard came riding up to their house. Maggie had not seen him since her return from Salem. Somehow he seemed much older than before.

"We heard about the sick girl," he said after he'd been invited to sit at their kitchen table. Cuyler ran to the study to call Father to join them.

"Father wants to know. . ." Richard began. "Well, I mean, actually, it was me who suggested it."

"Well, what is it, Richard?" Ethan said. "Can't you talk?"

The Allertons had never seen a Lankford at a loss for words.

"May we. . . May I invite Reverend Colman to come and pray with the girl?"

Maggie felt it was a strange request. No wonder he was tongue-tied. After all, they had Pastor Gee at North Church who was perfectly able to pray for folk. Why would they need the pastor of

133

the Brattle Street Church to come?

Her father once again surprised her by agreeing to the idea. "Please, Richard," he said, "do ask your pastor to come. And thank you for your kind consideration."

Martha was starting to set out mugs for cider, but Richard jumped up. "None for me please, Aunt Martha. I must go. I told Father I would be gone only a short time." He moved toward the door. "I'll get the message to the pastor right away, Dr. Allerton. Thank you."

After he was outside, Maggie turned to her father. "May I have permission to talk to Richard alone for a moment?"

Father smiled. "You have my permission."

Running out the door into the cool night air, Maggie called out to Richard, who was now astride his horse. "Richard? I've something to tell you."

Deftly, he swung out of the saddle and jumped down. "What is it, Maggie?"

"I have never apologized to you for my terrible behavior on Christmas afternoon. I was rude to you, and I'm sorry. Do you forgive me?"

"I never meant to cause you harm or embarrassment, Maggie. You had every right to be angry." In the soft moonlight she could see him smiling. "But I do accept your apology, and thank you for wanting to do so. I must hurry now." Quickly he remounted and was gone.

When the Reverend Colman arrived the next evening, he was not alone. Accompanying him was a tall, slender gentleman with the kindest eyes Maggie had ever seen. Reverend Colman introduced him as the Reverend Jonathan Edwards.

The infamous revivalist, Jonathan Edwards! Right in their house!

Maggie could hardly believe it. But he was nothing like all the wild stories she'd heard. He was dressed in plain clothing with his brown hair tied back at the neck.

Maggie glanced at Martha, who was smiling at her surprised expression. It was obvious Martha knew exactly who he was. Martha led the way to the nursery where Melee lay. "You go in first," Martha said to Maggie. "Make her understand these men are friends. We don't want her frightened all over again."

Because of Melee's trust in Maggie, no fear showed in her eyes as the men were allowed inside the room. Maggie listened as the soft-spoken Edwards explained in simple terms about Jesus' love and how He came from heaven to die for her sins.

Never had Maggie heard the plan of salvation explained in such a clear fashion. If this was what Mrs. Cradock and Aunt Ruth had heard preached, it was no wonder their lives were changed.

"Would you like to pray to become a child of God, Melee?" the Reverend Edwards was saying.

Melee was smiling and crying all at the same time. She placed her hands over her heart. "Loves Melee. Jesus loves Melee."

In halting broken English, Melee prayed a prayer of repentance with the Reverend Edwards. By the time they finished, everyone in the room was teary-eyed.

"You are now free in Jesus," the Reverend Edwards pronounced. "On the outside you may still be a slave, but on the inside you are free."

"Melee free," the girl repeated in awe. "Melee free."

In the following days, Martha moved a feather tick into the nursery so she could sleep on the floor next to Melee. Martha read Scriptures to Melee and recited Bible stories. Maggie worked doubly hard to keep the chores done in order to free Martha to be with Melee.

A few days following the pastor's visit, just before dawn, a knock sounded on Maggie's door. "Maggie, come quick," Martha said. "It's Melee. She's asking for you."

Maggie's heart pounded as she jumped down from her bed and ran down the hall toward the nursery.

Martha's face was somber. "Our young friend has taken a turn for the worse," she said.

"No! She can't." Maggie felt the breath go out of her. "She was getting better."

"Go to her," Martha said softly.

Maggie stepped nearer the bed to hear her name being called very softly. "Maggie, Maggie. Thank Maggie."

"I'm here, Melee. It's me, Maggie. I've come to be with you."

The dark eyes fluttered open, and a soft smile made Melee's face relax. She reached out her slender hand. Maggie took the hand, feeling its coolness.

"Maggie is friend." Maggie felt a slight squeeze on her hand. "No slave. Melee is free."

"Yes, Melee, you're free now." Maggie turned to look at Martha, who was weeping. "Get Father, Martha. Melee needs him."

"Right now, she needs you," Martha whispered. "Just you."

Maggie continued holding the hand and talking, just talking. Not knowing what to say, but talking anyway. Behind her, Martha prayed. Presently, the little hand went limp. When she felt it go, Maggie slumped across the bed, sobbing.

She lay there till the crying was all spent, then she felt Martha's strong arms lifting her up. She stood and allowed Martha to gather her into her arms and hold her as though she were a little girl again.

"Oh, Martha, Melee was so alone. I so wanted to help her go home."

"You did, my dear Maggie. You did. Melee's gone home. To her real home."

Spring arrived and worked its miracles on the countryside. Shade trees leafed out, flower gardens bloomed, the pastures were full of wildflowers, and even the air smelled differently. Long-legged colts and frisky white lambs leaped and played in the meadows. Maggie took in a long breath as though she were trying to drink fresh air deep into her lungs.

Richard laughed at her. "Don't breathe it all up," he said. "Save some for me."

Richard had invited her and Ethan to go horseback riding with him, and they'd taken turns racing without really caring who won. Now they were south of Boston Common, and the horses clopped along at a slower gait.

Three weeks had passed since they'd buried little Melee, and Maggie was only now beginning to feel like herself again. "I'm going to start a social work in the city," she was telling them.

"If anyone can do it, you can," Richard told her.

"What made you decide this?" Ethan asked.

"It was the first time I saw Ann Cradock on the dock last fall—when the other girls told me not to touch her. My heart ached, but I felt helpless."

She pulled her hood down off her head. Her red hair was loose and blowing, and it felt wonderful. "At first," she went on, "I shared my plan with Susannah, and she discouraged me."

"But you asked the wrong person," Richard offered.

"Exactly. Since then, I've talked to Martha, and she suggested I begin with people like Aunt Ruth, and like. . ." She looked over at Richard, who was smiling at her. "Like your mother."

"And what about Mrs. Cradock?" Ethan suggested. "I'd wager

she knows the needs of the common people."

"Why, you're right, of course, Ethan. What a marvelous idea."

Richard seemed to be leading the ride as they traveled on southward crossing through The Neck, the narrow strip of land which connected Boston to the mainland. This area, referred to by old-timers as "cow common" was full of rolling hills. As they came up over the brink of one of those hills, there before them lay a sight which made Maggie gasp. Thousands of people had gathered in carts, buggies, carriages, and on horseback—it could be only one thing.

"Richard, you've brought us to a revival meeting!" Maggie exclaimed. "You planned this all along."

"Very crafty," Ethan added.

"Your father is coming with Cuyler and Martha in the carriage later on," Richard said, smiling. "They're bringing along a lunch for us."

Maggie's defenses against the revivals had crumbled. After seeing the changes in Mrs. Cradock and Aunt Ruth and after meeting the kindly Jonathan Edwards, she was eager to hear the preaching. Soon her father arrived with Martha and Cuyler. They spread out blankets on the grassy hillside and shared a lunch. As the afternoon sun warmed the countryside, the outdoor congregation joined together in singing psalms. The glorious music ringing across the hillside sounded to Maggie like a choir of angels.

Soon the Reverend Jonathan Edwards came to the raised platform at the foot of the hill and began to preach. Many people around Maggie were crying and weeping openly, but there were none of the wild gyrations she'd heard about.

With a hungry heart, Maggie listened to the words that clearly explained God's love and mercy. The truth was clear to her now.

She was responsible for her own decision to make Jesus her Lord.

Later, as the rosy dusk marked the closing of the momentous day, the crowds began to break up. As Maggie helped to fold the blankets, she heard a voice calling her name. She turned about to see Dancy running toward her.

"Oh, Maggie, you're here, too." Dancy ran up and gave Maggie a hug. "It's nothing like we thought, is it? I'm so ashamed of all our senseless scoffing."

"We spoke in our ignorance, Dancy, but now we know the truth." The look of peace in Dancy's eyes told Maggie that she indeed knew the Truth as well.

"Mother and Father have brought me out for nearly every meeting. I've invited Susannah to come as well, but she only laughs at me."

"We can pray for her," Maggie said. "God is faithful to answer our prayers."

"I know that now."

"Dancy," Maggie said, "I am thinking of starting a work in Boston to assist those less fortunate. I don't know exactly how to begin, but I'm trusting the Lord to guide me. Would you consider becoming a part of the work?"

"Oh, Maggie, what an unselfish plan. We laughed at you when you spoke of helping the girl named Ann. I am sorry now that I laughed. I'm sure Mother would like to be a part as well," she added. "I must go now. They're waiting for me. Goodbye, Maggie." She ran a ways down the hill, then called back, "I'm so glad we're sisters in the Lord."

A cool breeze had come up, softly ruffling the leaves in the trees. One of the first stars winked overhead. As she walked along with her family, Maggie felt warm and content to the very depths of her soul.

"Let me take that," Richard said, lifting the heavy blanket from her arms. Then he boldly grasped her hand as they strolled to the carriage together.

Good News for Readers

The American Adventure continues with *Boston Revolts*. The year is 1764 and Boston's streets are filled with violence. Angry because of increasing taxes, mobs are attacking British agents and soldiers. They burn homes and destroy property. Even people who are forced to house British soldiers are not safe from the mob's fury.

William and Kathleen Lankford, the children of Maggie and Richard, watch in horror as a young British soldier is shot right in front of them. Their Uncle Cuyler, a doctor, wants them to help him treat the soldier. But if they do, what will the mob do to them? And what will happen to their family's home?

You're in for the ultimate
American Adventure!
Collect all 48 books!